"What if I spend some time with Gracie, just to clear up this daddy notion of hers?" Wyatt asked.

"In exchange for what?" Ellie's eyes searched his face.

"For you watching my son for a few hours. I know I'm getting the better deal, but Gracie obviously needs someone to talk to. And I need help with Cade."

"But the evenings, before bedtime, those are special daddy moments you shouldn't miss with Cade," she protested.

"Something has to give, Ellie." He hated admitting that. "I have to work and keep our home up."

"I have just one condition," Ellie said.

"Name it."

"You have to agree that this is simply an arrangement between friends and nothing more. I'm not looking for a father for Gracie or a relationship for myself. I need you to be clear on that, Wyatt. Strictly friends."

"Agreed," he said with a nod, relief swelling. "I don't want any romantic entanglements, either." He grinned at her and thrust out his hand. "Deal, friend?"

Ellie took her time but finally she shook hands with him. "Deal."

Lois Richer loves traveling, swimming and quilting, but mostly she loves writing stories that show God's boundless love for His precious children. As she says, "His love never changes or gives up. It's always waiting for me. My stories feature imperfect characters learning that love doesn't mean attaining perfection. Love is about keeping on keeping on." You can contact Lois via email, loisricher@yahoo.com, or on Facebook (loisricherauthor).

Books by Lois Richer

Love Inspired

Wranglers Ranch

The Rancher's Family Wish
Her Christmas Family Wish

Family Ties

A Dad for Her Twins
Rancher Daddy
Gift-Wrapped Family
Accidental Dad

Northern Lights

North Country Hero
North Country Family
North Country Mom
North Country Dad

Healing Hearts

A Doctor's Vow
Yuletide Proposal
Perfectly Matched

Visit the Author Profile page at Harlequin.com for more titles.

Ch.F.

Her Christmas Family Wish

Lois Richer

Recycling programs for this product may not exist in your area.

ISBN-13: 978-0-373-81950-8

Her Christmas Family Wish

This edition published by arrangement with Love Inspired Books.

www.Harlequin.com

Printed in U.S.A.

Whatever your hands find to do,
do it with your might.
—*Ecclesiastes* 9:10

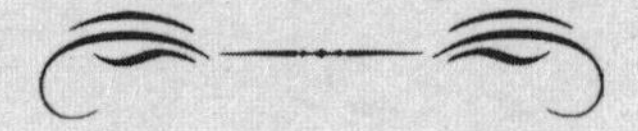

This book is dedicated to my nephew Drew,
who is on the way to discovering his future.
God bless you, Drew.

Chapter One

"That little boy would be a good brother, wouldn't he, Mommy?"

Wyatt Wright stifled his groan. Not another one. He'd been in this grocery story almost twenty minutes, and he'd put only three things from his list into his basket, thanks to his son's many female admirers. At least, that's how he preferred to think of the women who used Cade to open a conversation with him.

Only this time Cade's fan sounded like a little kid.

"He's a cutie all ri—" A woman's light, cheery voice paused. "Uh-oh."

Intrigued by the way warning overtook her amusement, Wyatt did something he'd vowed not to. He looked directly at the stranger and spoke to her.

"Is something wrong?"

She peered at Cade. "Your son is about to be sick."

Clear gray eyes set in a heart-shaped face met his, empty of the coy look he often saw in the ladies who were—how did he say it without sounding conceited?—looking to make his acquaintance. And yet Wyatt didn't get the impression that he was the attraction here, given the coolly polite smile that lifted this woman's pink lips. Still, he couldn't help but admire her flaxen hair as it tumbled to her shoulders in an attractive disarray of curls. She wore a pale blue sundress, probably in deference to the heat of a late-October evening in Tucson, that flirted around her tanned legs.

Cade was sick? That was an opening gambit he hadn't heard before. Of course she was wrong. Wyatt had been eighteen-month-old Cade's sole parent for over a year. He knew all about—

"Look out!" the pretty stranger warned.

Wyatt turned in time to see his usually grinning boy grimace before spewing a sour mouthful all over his daddy's favorite T-shirt.

"Sorry. I tried to warn you." The slender stranger was quite tall, only a few inches shorter than Wyatt's own six-foot height. She dug into her large shoulder bag, pulled out a packet of wipes and extracted several. "Poor baby. But your tummy feels better now, doesn't it?"

Wyatt blinked twice before realizing her tender tone was for Cade. Gently she wiped the disgusting mess from his son's face and shirtfront, then tucked the used wipes into a plastic bag which she grabbed from a roll at the nearby produce stand. After removing more clean wipes, she reached toward Wyatt. He stepped back just in time to stop her from cleaning him up, too.

"Oh. Sorry." She blushed very prettily, then stuffed the wipes into his hand. "I guess you can do that yourself. Moms get used to cleaning up spills. But I suppose dads do, too, right?"

Entranced by the melodic sound of her light laugh, Wyatt couldn't find his voice. After a minute her smile faded. She shrugged, then bent to look at Cade.

"Hope you feel better, sweet boy." Cade grinned at her, his feet churning. She glanced at Wyatt. "You've got a real charmer here." Then she turned and reached for her daughter's hand. "Come on, Gracie."

Wyatt hid his smile when the little girl planted her feet and stubbornly refused to move.

"This man would make a good daddy for us, Mommy," the blue-eyed sprite mused, her silvery-gold head tilted as she assessed Wyatt.

That was so *not* funny. Wyatt suppressed his overwhelming desire to bolt.

"Then he—" Gracie continued jerking a thumb at Cade "—could be my brother. I'd really like to have a brother," she added, her head tilted to one side thoughtfully. Then she frowned. "'Cept I don't want him to spit on me."

Wyatt cleared his throat, intending to voice a firm yet delicate refusal that would end the child's ludicrous notion real fast, before her mother latched on to it. Instead he got side-tracked by the lady's burst of laughter.

"You used to spit up exactly the same way, Gracie." The mom chuckled when her daughter wrinkled her nose in disgust. "But we don't need a daddy," she said in a firm voice. "We're fine just the way we are, you and me. Don't you like our family?"

Instead of rushing her child away from a touchy subject, as Wyatt had seen other parents do, the mother waited for a response. He admired her serenity and total focus on her child and made a mental note to practice the same kind of patience with Cade when he got older so he'd be the best father a kid could have. He'd do whatever it took to be a better father to his son than his own father had ever been.

"Our family's nice," Gracie agreed. "But I want a daddy. And a brother. Melissa and Courtney have brothers and daddies," she said, her chin thrust up.

"So you've told me, many times." A resigned sigh colored the mother's response. "But I'm sure there are other kids in your kindergarten class who don't. Each family is different, Gracie. One isn't better or worse than another, just different." She smoothed the child's rumpled curls. "We need to get our ice cream now so we can go to Wranglers Ranch."

Wranglers Ranch? That was the place that sponsored camps for troubled kids. Months earlier the owner, Tanner Johns, had left a message on Wyatt's answering machine asking him if he was interested in taking on a full-time vet position there. Wyatt, his hands full caring for Cade, hadn't responded. Though he kept running into Tanner at church, the rancher had never pressed him for a reply, simply offered friendship. Wyatt figured Wranglers' ministry must be growing because of a mention at last week's church service about a youth group outing to the ranch.

"And—" Gracie dragged out the word, giving him and Cade another once-over before blowing out a heartfelt sigh. "Now that Beth and Davy live at Wranglers Ranch, they have a daddy, too. I'm the only one who doesn't."

The pathos in her mournful words reached in

and squeezed Wyatt's heart, until he caught the mother's grimace as she rolled her eyes at him.

"Oh, that's not the worst of my shortcomings," she explained with a teasing chuckle. "Last week Gracie was the *only one* in her kindergarten class not allowed to stay up late to watch a TV show." She raised her eyebrows in a pseudo-severe look. "As you must know, single parenthood isn't for the faint of heart." She fluttered her fingers. "We have to go. Bye."

Wyatt nodded bemusedly until her gaze dropped to his shirt.

"You, uh, might want to get that off before it dries," she advised quietly. Then she took Gracie's hand and firmly drew her toward the freezer section.

Wyatt grimaced and used the wad of wipes she'd handed him to clean up the mess as best he could.

"Thanks a lot," he said to his son who was now happily blowing bubbles.

Wyatt quickly gathered the rest of the items on his list and hurried through the checkout determined to avoid another encounter with more of Cade's admirers. But in the parking lot he noticed the same woman buckling her little girl into a car seat. Pure impulse and an innate curiosity he should have suppressed sent Wyatt walking briskly toward them.

"How did you know?" he asked abruptly.

The woman jerked in surprise, bumping her head on the car before she ducked out.

"Ow!" She raised a slim arm to rub the top of her head. "Sorry?" Her eyebrows drew together as she frowned at him.

"How did you know Cade was going to be sick?" Wyatt repeated.

"Years of pediatric nursing and a child of my own," she explained with a shrug. "It's the kind of look I learned to interpret fast and clean up faster." She checked out his shirt. "Good job. Did you feed him something new for lunch?"

"A couple of brussels sprouts," he admitted. "He seemed okay with them."

"Ew! I'm afraid I'd have the same reaction as he did. Not my favorite vegetable." She shrugged at Wyatt's frown. "Well, sorry, but it's not."

"Rounded nutrition is the best thing for kids," he repeated, quoting verbatim from the baby book he used as his parenting mentor.

The woman opened her lips to say something but was interrupted.

"What's that boy's name?" Gracie asked, poking her head forward.

"He's Cade. I'm Wyatt. Wyatt Wright," he said, shocked that he was voluntarily giving his name to a child and her mother—a single woman, to boot. But there was something about this woman that drew him. Because she was attractive? Compelling? Intriguing?

All of the above.

"We're Ellie and Gracie Grant. But I already know who you are, Wyatt." Ellie laughed at his surprise. "I've seen you at church. In fact, you're the current hot topic."

"I am?" He frowned at her. "Why?"

"Mmm." She tapped her forefinger against her lips. "How can I put this delicately? Let's just say there are a lot of single ladies at our church who feel you've been a widower too long, that you need a good woman to help you with this little guy."

Aghast, Wyatt stood frozen as Ellie chucked Cade under the chin. Cade's giggle was Wyatt's favorite sound because it made him feel like he wasn't the awful failure his own father had been.

He wasn't sure how to reply, though he wanted to ask Ellie if she was one of *those* ladies from church. Not that it mattered. Wyatt doubted that even knowing she was would end the zip of electricity curling up his spine.

"Don't worry, Wyatt." That thread of laughter lilted through Ellie's voice. She winked at him. "You're safe with me."

"I am?" Wyatt gulped down a rush of disappointment. Hey! Shouldn't he be feeling relief?

"Yep, very safe." Ellie checked that Gracie

was secure, then carefully closed the car door, maybe so her daughter couldn't overhear? "Despite Gracie's comments, I am not on the hunt for a husband. Raising Gracie takes all my focus. I'm not interested in romance," she said airily, though he heard a bit of an edge to the words.

Wyatt didn't have time to ask why a gorgeous woman like her wouldn't want love in her life because she walked around the car and pulled open the front door. She tossed him a funny, almost sad smile, then climbed inside and drove away.

"Well," he said to Cade as he pushed the grocery cart toward his car. "That was interesting. But don't do the sick part again, okay? It makes us both smell bad. Got it?"

Cade crowed his agreement as if he knew that the encounter with that remarkable woman and her daughter had made his daddy's day brighter.

While Wyatt fastened Cade in his seat, then loaded the groceries, his thoughts replayed his interaction with the mother-daughter duo. He'd liked them both, but he especially liked Ellie's forthrightness.

Wait a minute!

"Focus on parenthood," he ordered his wayward brain. "You're a single dad with a veterinarian practice that barely supports you and a ranch that needs tons of work and money."

It's up to you, Wyatt, to use your business to

follow in my footsteps and make the Wright name stand out in this town. His father's last words brought the same rush of irritation and burst of inferiority that they had the day Bernard Wright had said them ten years ago.

Wyatt glanced in the mirror at his son.

"Can't focus on that right now, Dad," he muttered as he drove home. "Taryn's gone. I'm the only one Cade has. I have to be here for him." *The way I wasn't there for Taryn.*

A tinder of unforgiveness flamed anew at the memory of his wife's needless death. Yes, the underage teens who hit her were guilty. But so was Wyatt. Taryn shouldn't have been driving that night. Wyatt had promised her that morning that he'd pick up diapers and formula for Cade by lunchtime, but he'd forgotten. Later he'd promised Taryn he'd do it on his way home from a call, but he'd forgotten again. After dinner and another promise that he'd make a run to the grocery store when he'd finished his coffee, he'd fallen asleep with Cade on his chest, failing to remember his promise. So Taryn had let him sleep and gone herself.

His wife had been killed. Because of him.

Familiar guilt gnawed at Wyatt as he pulled into his driveway. He'd made promises he hadn't kept, disappointed his wife and, worse, left her alone day after day to fulfill dreams for the ranch they'd planned to restore together while he pursued the goal of making his veterinary business number one in Tucson. Wyatt had failed his wife miserably.

And why? Because he couldn't forget that deathbed promise to his father. He'd worked eighteen hours a day, taken on every client who called, hoping he could somehow prove himself worthy of the prestigious Wright name. But that time had been stolen from Taryn. Wasn't it silly that even now, alone, a single parent and almost thirty years old, Wyatt still couldn't shed his long-buried need to prove himself worthy of his father's love?

Losing Taryn had taught him one hard lesson. Don't make promises you can't keep. His father had taught him the other. Never make Cade feel he had to earn his daddy's love.

Wyatt carried his now-sleeping child into the house and settled him before retrieving his groceries and storing them. He would still make his father proud; it was just going to take a little longer. Because now Cade came first, before his practice, before the ranch, before the promise to his father, before anything.

Ellie's sweet laugh filled Wyatt's head, and for a moment he wished— No! He ruthlessly pushed her lovely face from his mind and started on the laundry. There was no way he'd let another woman in his life and risk failing her the way he had Taryn.

No way at all.

"He was a nice daddy, wasn't he, Mommy?" Gracie chirped from the backseat. "I liked Cade, too." She paused. Ellie saw her wrinkle her nose. "'Cept when he got sick. That was gross."

"Gross? Where did you hear that?" Ellie asked, one eyebrow raised.

"Melissa. Can I play with the horses at Wranglers Ranch?" Gracie asked in a quick change of topic.

"I don't think so, honey. The horses are probably ready to sleep now." Ellie hoped so, because she was too tired to deal with a wiggling, shrieking Gracie astride a horse.

She drove toward Wranglers Ranch, smiling as she remembered Wranglers' slogan. *You're always welcome here*. She did feel at home there, and she loved her job as camp nurse.

"I thought you wanted to play with Beth and Davy?" she reminded Gracie, lest her daughter get fixated on dreams of horse riding.

"I *do* want to play with them. And invite them to my birthday party." Gracie's forehead furrowed as she fell into thought. "How many days is it until my birthday, Mommy?"

"You'll be six in about three more weeks, right

after Thanksgiving." Ellie bit her lip as worry about that birthday party built inside her. "Did you think of something you'd specially like for your birthday, honey?"

After Gracie's birth, Ellie had started a day care to enable her to stay home with her child. But outgoing, curious Gracie now needed more, and so did her mother. So late in the summer Ellie had closed the day care and enrolled Gracie in kindergarten. That's why she'd taken the job at Wranglers Ranch—so she could still be with kids. Ellie loved kids.

Tanner Johns had told her that the government had awarded him a big new contract to work with troubled youth, with one caveat—Wranglers Ranch must have a nurse on the premises when their youth groups attended. Tanner had offered Ellie the job one day after church, and since she was eager to return to the profession she'd originally left to care for her sick sister, Ellie gladly accepted. She'd started working at Wranglers in mid-September and never regretted her choice.

"I already told you what I want for my birthday, 'member?" A glance in the rearview mirror revealed Gracie's arms firmly crossed over her small chest. "I want a daddy."

"Honey, I can't give you a daddy for your

birthday. Or at all," Ellie said for what seemed the hundredth time. "I've told you that before."

"But why?" Gracie's bottom lip jutted out.

"Because." Ellie stifled her exasperation. How long would the child keep constantly asking for a father? What was she doing wrong that Gracie wasn't happy with *her*? "Nobody can give daddies for birthdays, sweetheart."

"For Christmas, then? That's far away. That's lots of time to get him," Gracie wheedled.

"I can't get you a daddy for Christmas either," Ellie replied in her firmest voice.

"But I need one!" Gracie burst into tears.

Ellie heaved a sigh, wishing there was some way to meet and marry the perfect man who would give her daughter her dream.

You tried love. Look how that turned out. Gracie would have been left out in the cold.

Gracie sniffed and Ellie winced. Never did she feel more helpless, less capable of being a parent than when her daughter wept.

God? I'm new at this praying stuff. Will You help me? I don't know what to say. I don't want to break Gracie's heart, but I know now that marriage isn't part of Your plan for me.

"Honey, things like daddies and mommies and baby brothers or sisters are up to God." Ellie didn't know how else to put it. "I guess

He thinks that we're doing okay together, just the two of us."

"I'm gonna keep praying." Gracie's chin thrust out. "Because we *need* a daddy."

"Gracie, you know I love you very much," Ellie said helplessly, "that I couldn't love you more."

"I know." Gracie watched as they drove through the gates on to Wranglers Ranch. "But I want a daddy to love me, too."

"But, honey—"

"I'm going to ask God to give us Cade and his daddy," Gracie said with resolute firmness.

"You can't!" Aghast, Ellie braked in front of the ranch house a little too hard as she scoured her brain for some way to dissuade Gracie. Only her daughter wasn't listening.

"I can, too, pray, Mommy. I can pray to God for anything. That's what Pastor Jeff said." Gracie's chin thrust out in unyielding determination. "And I'm going to pray for that."

"But—but—" Exasperated, Ellie fell silent. After all, hadn't she taken Gracie to church hoping she'd start learning more about *her Father*? Oh, dear.

"Hey, there's Beth, and she's holding a baby bunny." In a flash Gracie forgot about daddies, snapped off her seat belt and bolted out of the car. She was running across the yard before Ellie could stop her. "When did they come, Beth?" she shouted in her most excited voice. "Can I hold one?"

"You don't look happy." Tanner Johns, her boss, pulled open her car door, waiting until Ellie had climbed out before he asked, "What's the matter?"

"What else? Gracie. She won't give up on getting a father. And now she's found a candidate." Ellie grimaced, though she couldn't deny Gracie's choice was very handsome.

"Who's the chosen guy?" Tanner took the ice cream from her as they strolled to his front door.

"Someone we met at the grocery store tonight. You probably know him." Ellie preceded Tanner into the house and waited for that speculative glint to appear in her friend Sophie's eyes as Tanner explained the gist of the conversation to his wife.

"Yes, who is Gracie's choice for a daddy?" Sophie asked with a smile as she turned from speaking to their friend Moses.

"Wyatt Wright." Ellie sighed. "Gracie says she's going to pray God will give her Wyatt for a dad and his son, Cade, for her brother."

"We all know Wyatt," Tanner said. "He's the veterinarian I've been hoping would take on Wranglers Ranch as a client. But I get the impression he doesn't feel he can handle our business right now."

"He seems like a great parent, though he missed the signs that Cade was about to be sick." Ellie made a face. "Wyatt fed him brussels sprouts," she told Sophie, who laughed.

"Maybe he's still learning about kids," Tanner defended. "But Wyatt is an expert on horses. The man has a first-rate reputation. About two years ago his practice was the most sought after in Tucson, but then his wife died shortly after Cade was born." He shook his head. "Whenever we talk at church Wyatt's totally focused on being a dad."

Moses was an elderly Native American who'd cared for and nurtured the abused horses that Wranglers Ranch took in and had lived here long before Tanner had taken over. Now he nodded his head in agreement.

"The Double M tried to hire him, too." Moses had a soft spot for anyone who loved horses as much as he did. "Heard Wyatt told them no, said he had to focus on his son and that work came second."

"Nice if you can afford it," Ellie murmured, thinking of her own years when Gracie was a baby and how she'd struggled to manage on her shoestring budget.

"Wyatt's a good-looking man, don't you think, Ellie?" Sophie's gaze trapped her.

"Yes, he's very handsome," Ellie managed to say while her brain mocked her tepid appreciation of that very attractive man. "But I'm not interested."

"Why not? He certainly seems to be the focus of the ladies' groups at church." Sophie scooped the ice cream Ellie had brought onto steaming slices of her fresh peach pie. "Moses, didn't you tell me Lucy Marten asked Wyatt to dinner last week?" She glanced at the old man, one eyebrow arched. "What's the news on that?"

"Heard he turned her down like he does all those females. Anyone can see they're just itching to get their hands on him. Prize catch, a guy like that." Moses grinned as he held out a hand to take his pie. "Thank you, Sophie." He lifted a forkful to his lips, then closed his eyes as he savored the dessert. "Excellent," he proclaimed a moment later. "No wonder we always have kids showing up here to eat. With cooking like this on offer, why wouldn't they?"

"You're very sweet, Moses." When Sophie patted his cheek Ellie could almost hear the crusty old man's gruff demeanor crumble. Then the children arrived and demanded some pie. As they devoured it, Sophie asked Ellie if Gracie could play with her kids, Beth and Davy, for a while longer.

"Yeah, why don't you stay, Ellie?" Tanner offered. He winked. "We can talk about Wyatt some more if you like."

"No need. I told you I'm not interested." Ellie pretended an airiness she didn't feel. "But since it's Friday and there's no school tomorrow, I guess we could stay awhile." She chuckled at Gracie's whoop of excitement as all three kids scampered into Beth's room to play with the amazing dollhouse Tanner had given her last Christmas.

"Hard to believe it will soon be that time again," he marveled with a fond look at Sophie. "What do you want this Christmas?" he asked as her hand slid into his.

"I have everything I want," she murmured.

"Good answer." Tanner leaned over to press a kiss against her cheek. "This has been a wonderful year for Wranglers Ranch and us."

"Your dream that this ranch would be a haven for homeless and needy kids is coming true with every child we reach." Sophie hugged his side. "We're blessed to have such wonderful helpers like Moses and Ellie and all the hands."

"Now if I could just find a way to persuade Wyatt to come on staff," Tanner murmured before he held out his plate for seconds.

Sophie dished up another piece of pie then turned to Ellie. "Maybe you could talk to Wyatt for us, tell him how much we'd love to have him working here on the ranch."

"Me?" Ellie shook her head. "I barely know the man."

"That's easily rectified," Sophie pointed out.

"Don't go there, Sophie," Ellie warned. "I'm glad you and Tanner found each other and that you're happy together. But I learned the hard way that romance isn't for me."

"But—" Sophie stopped when Ellie shook her head.

"I made a bad mistake when I let myself fall in love with Eddie. If I'd known him as well as I thought, I'd have known he'd change after he inherited that money, that he wouldn't want to be saddled with being a father to Gracie." A wiggle of pain still festered inside. "But I didn't really know him because I was too busy thinking that my silly dream of a big, happy family was finally coming true."

"Nothing silly about that dream, girlie," Moses piped up. "God gave us families."

"I know. And I have Gracie. That's enough." She saw Sophie was about to speak and shook her head. "Listen, when I got involved with Eddie I took my focus off parenting Gracie, and she almost paid for it. We were only a few weeks away from getting married when he suggested I put her in boarding school." The memory still made her flinch. "I don't need to repeat my mistakes. God's given me the job of raising my daughter and I'll focus on that. I guess I'm like Wyatt in that way. My child comes first."

Later, as Ellie drove home with Gracie sleeping in the backseat, her brain revived a mental image of Wyatt Wright. He was good-looking, interesting and seemed to be a great parent, but he wasn't for her.

Gracie was just going to have to ask God for something else, because Ellie had no intention of including Wyatt, or his very cute son, in their lives. Her broken engagement had proven that being a single mom had to be her number-one priority. Maybe someday, when Gracie was grown up and on her own, maybe then Ellie could consider a relationship.

Maybe.

But not now.

Chapter Two

"You're making a lot of noise for a kid who's been fed, watered and changed."

In the year since Taryn's death Wyatt had grown comfortable speaking to Cade as if he understood everything. What he doubted he'd ever get used to was the volume of noise a small child could generate.

"You'll give me a bad reputation as a dad," he complained as he drove into Wranglers Ranch.

While Cade, red-faced and bellowing, continued his vocal outrage, Wyatt parked beside the visitors sign and exited the noisy truck with a sigh of relief.

"Nothing wrong with his lungs, is there?" Tanner appeared and held out a hand. "Nice to see you again, Wyatt."

"You, too, Tanner." He shook hands then picked up Cade. "He's in a bad mood because he wouldn't settle for his nap." He offered a soother, but Cade knocked it from his hand.

"Got a temper, too." Tanner laughed as he bent and picked it up.

"I'm sorry about this," he said as Cade launched into another earsplitting roar. "I did warn you I couldn't get a sitter." Wyatt jiggled the grumpy child in a futile hope that he'd relax and perhaps drift off to sleep. "Maybe you should get another vet."

"Don't want anyone else," Tanner said firmly. "You have the best reputation around these parts when it comes to horses, Wyatt. I want *your* opinion."

"Okay. On what?"

"Two animals I'm considering buying." Tanner winced as Cade amped up his protests. "Come on. We'll take him to Sophie. She'll know what to do."

Wyatt desperately hoped so. He'd been through Cade's overtired days before, and though his son eventually relaxed and fell asleep, the experience always left *him* drained.

But his hopes were dashed when he heard someone say, "I'm sorry, Tanner, but Sophie went shopping. She's catering that barbecue tonight, remember?"

Wyatt turned and saw her. The woman from the grocery store.

Though Ellie smiled as she approached the Wranglers' boss, Wyatt thought her face tensed when her gaze moved to him. "Hello, again," she said in a pleasant tone.

"Hi. Sorry about the racket." He shifted Cade from one hip to the other. "How's Gracie?"

"She's fine. May I take him?" Ellie held out her hands with a smile. "Hello there, little man," she said in that lilting voice he hadn't been able to forget. "What's your issue?"

Cade stopped midscreech to stare at her. Then he grinned and clapped his hands.

"Traitor." The word slipped out without thinking. Embarrassed, Wyatt caught Ellie's grin. "He missed his nap."

"And he's been taking it out on you." She laughed and nodded. "Been there. Why don't you leave him with me? I'll rock him on the porch for a few minutes, and he'll soon nod off." She studied Cade's now-drooping eyes. "See? I doubt he'll be awake long."

"Maybe," Wyatt said doubtfully. "But that's too much of an imposition. This is your workplace." He held out his hands. "I'll just take him home. Maybe I can make it back another time, if you really want my advice," he said to Tanner.

"Please, leave him. I'd enjoy the break. The morning's been a little monotonous." Ellie winked at Tanner. "No kids have fallen off their horse or skinned a knee, so I've been a bit bored."

"Our guests do not *fall off*," Tanner protested indignantly.

"Sorry. Of course they don't. It's all to do with gravity." Ellie winked at Wyatt. "Seriously, we'll be fine. I'll call Tanner if I need you."

Wyatt hesitated, watching her face soften as she swayed back and forth with Cade. His son's eyes were almost closed, his thumb in his mouth. "You're sure?" he murmured.

"Positive." Ellie began to hum softly while maintaining the same swaying movements. A tiny smile flirted with her lips. "Walk away now," she sing-songed, never losing a beat in her lullaby.

Since Taryn's death Wyatt had trusted his son to only two sitters and then only after a complete vetting by him and Tucson's premier child care agency. Yet somehow he felt utterly confident in Ellie's abilities with Cade. Maybe it was because he'd seen her with Gracie and knew her to be a loving parent. Or maybe it was the way she so confidently held Cade that he immediately relaxed in her arms.

"You can trust Ellie," Tanner added.

"I know." Wyatt set down the diaper bag he held. "Here's his stuff."

Ellie's gaze met his, a knowing look in her gray eyes. "I promise he'll be all right."

Of course he would. Because, thanks to Ellie, Cade was already sleeping.

"I'll be back in about an hour," he said.

"We'll be here." Ellie's smile lent encouragement as he went on his way.

As it turned out, Wyatt's inspection of Tanner's horses went slowly, thorough as it was.

"These mares appear healthy and well cared for. They should be fine to breed." Wyatt stretched his back, his examination finally complete. "I'll run the blood samples anyway, but I doubt there's an issue." He frowned, noting a larger, older stallion in the paddock beyond. "Him I'm not so sure about. Where'd you get him?"

"He was left here late last night." Tanner's lips tightened. "I'm guessing he's been kept inside a barn or something for a long time, because I'm pretty sure he's got thrush on his feet."

"That's not a common ailment here in the desert." Wyatt climbed the fence and walked closer for a better look, barely aware that Tanner followed. "He seems lame… Did you notice he doesn't flex his foot?" He spoke soothingly while he lifted the horse's leg and probed the tender heel and frog area.

"Yeah, I noticed. Lack of flexing usually means his hooves didn't get cleaned much." Tanner's voice was low and gruff. "Which certainly seems to be the case."

"It's hard to understand cruelty to animals," Wyatt agreed softly. "You're doing the right thing. Keep him in the fresh air, get him to walk around, and watch what happens."

"Can I call you if it doesn't clear up?"

"Of course. Meanwhile, keep his heels trimmed back." Wyatt swept his hand across the horse's flanks after releasing his foot. "He could stand some extra oats, too."

"He's getting them," Tanner said with a nod. "Don't worry, Wyatt. My foreman, Lefty, Moses and I are all keeping a close eye on this guy. He won't suffer at Wranglers."

"You've got some great stock here, the kind I'd like to add to my own ranch someday." Wyatt surveyed the other horses with their shiny coats in the surrounding paddocks. Someday, he promised himself as he closed the gate. Then he wondered if he could keep that promise.

"You're anxious to get back to Cade." Tanner wasn't asking a question.

Wyatt nodded. "I used to be a workaholic, but after Taryn died, I vowed I'd always put Cade first." Self-conscious about revealing that, Wyatt kept his head bent as he cleaned his boots on the grass.

"A good thing for all fathers to remember," Tanner agreed. "But doing your job isn't ignoring Cade. He's not suffering. He's probably still sleeping, in fact. And he's got an amazing caregiver in Ellie. She's really fantastic with kids. She used to have lists of people begging to get their kids into her day care."

"It was nice of her to watch him for me." So Ellie had run a day care. Was that how she'd known Cade was going to be sick that day in the store? "I thought she was a nurse."

"She is. But when Gracie was born, Ellie wanted to stay home with her. So she set up a day care in her house." Tanner made a face. "Believe me, there were a lot of unhappy folks last August when she closed down Fiddlesticks—that was the name of her day care."

"If it was successful, why would she do that?" He had no business asking anything about Wranglers' nurse, but Wyatt was curious.

"Gracie was ready for school. Ellie figured it was a good time to get back to nursing." He grinned. "Sophie and I have been blessed having her here at Wranglers. The kids just adore her. Cade will, too. You'll see."

Privately Wyatt doubted his son would be around Ellie Grant enough to get to that stage, but he simply nodded and kept his opinions to himself, anxious to see how his son had fared.

"He's still asleep," Ellie said meeting them at the patio door. "I've just made some coffee and put a tray out here. Want some?"

"Sounds good. I see Sophie's car. I'll just go see if she needs help," Tanner said. "You two go ahead."

Somewhat self-consciously Wyatt followed Ellie to the table under a lacy mesquite tree where she'd set a plate of cookies, a carafe and three mugs. Cade lay nearby in the shade in a makeshift bed in an old washtub, eyes closed, breathing deeply.

"He's still sleeping." Wyatt was somewhat surprised to realize two hours had passed.

"Of course." Ellie smiled, her eyes lighting up as she glanced at the little boy. "He wore himself out yelling, I guess. Gracie used to do that. Drove me bonkers sometimes. She'd get so tired out that she couldn't seem to relax and let sleep come. I was usually so exhausted that when she finally crashed I did, too."

"Except when you had to open your day care," he added. "Tanner said you had a long client list."

"I did. It was fun if exhausting. I was ready for a change. Especially after—" She checked herself as a fleeting frown washed over her face, then regrouped and shrugged. "I was pretty nervous about letting Gracie start school."

"Why?" He sipped the coffee she'd poured.

"Until then I'd been in total control of Gracie's world." Her lips tilted in a wry smile. "The thought of allowing someone else to take over and not be there to see she was all right caused me some sleepless nights."

"So how did you handle it?" he asked.

"With Sophie's help." Ellie grinned. "I'd consulted her about some catering, she led me to the Lord, and she's been mentoring me ever since. She suggested I needed to start trusting that God cares as much and even more about Gracie than I do, so now I'm trying to trust Him. Since I'm a control freak where Gracie's concerned it's not easy, but I'm learning."

"Was Sophie catering something for your day care?" he asked as he selected one of Sophie's homemade cookies from the plate Ellie held out.

"Uh, no." Ellie hesitated. To Wyatt she looked sort of embarrassed. "Something personal, but it turned out that I didn't need her services after all." Her diffidence surprised him.

"She sure has a good reputation as a caterer. Well deserved, judging by these cookies." He savored the lemon flavor. "I've heard about her success all over Tucson." Wyatt glanced around.

"Just like I've heard about Tanner's success with this place."

"Sophie's amazing, and Wranglers Ranch is a fantastic ministry. I am so happy to be part of it," Ellie enthused. "And Gracie loves school, so God took care of that worry, too." She studied him, her head tilted to one side. "How do you manage work and Cade?"

"Mostly I don't," Wyatt admitted. "My wife died about a year ago. Since then work has come a distant second."

"I'm sure." She touched his hand fleetingly. "I'm sorry, Wyatt."

"Thanks. Anyway, I'm Cade's only parent now, so I've been trying to be sure I'm there when he needs me." He made a face. "Only thing is, toddlers don't have much downtime. And that makes it hard to build up my veterinarian practice."

"And you must do that—build it up?" Ellie's eyebrows lifted as she waited.

"Yes. It's very important to me." He wasn't going to tell her why, though he could see the question lurking in her eyes. "But it's difficult. Just yesterday I agreed to be at a client's place in the morning, but then Cade bumped his head on the coffee table. After that he wouldn't settle down, so I had to cancel." He made a face. "Doesn't make for a good working relationship with your clients or help your reputation when you have to withdraw from a call."

"No, I don't suppose it does." Ellie frowned. "Couldn't you hire a caregiver to come in?"

"I do sometimes," he said, feeling defensive. "But she wasn't available yesterday morning when I called."

"I can see that would be a problem. What about scheduling specific work hours? You could hire a caregiver from, say, eight to noon. While they watched Cade you could work, knowing you'd be available for him later."

"Actually I did try that once when Cade was younger. It didn't work." Wyatt reconsidered. "Maybe it's time to try it again. Thanks." The agency would be relieved if he had regular hours to offer their nannies instead of always calling at the last minute.

"Now, since I've helped you, would you be willing to help me out?" she asked with a cheeky grin.

"Uh, with what?" he asked. Depending on what she wanted, he might have to refuse her. He wasn't getting involved.

"I had this idea that Wranglers should sponsor a Thanksgiving Day dinner for kids who don't have any place to go." Ellie huffed out a sigh that lifted the spiky bangs across her forehead. "Of course Sophie will do the food, but she and

Tanner asked me to set up some kind of decorations and, well…" She made a face. "I'm not exactly artistic. The most art I've ever done is kids' crafts at my day care."

"Why not go with that?" Wyatt shrugged. "Wranglers is a kids' camp, after all."

"How exactly would that work?" Ellie stared at him as if he had all the answers.

And that was so far from the truth that Wyatt wanted to laugh. He had the answers to exactly nothing in his own life. How could he possibly help anyone else?

"Come on, tell me what you were thinking," she pressed.

He tried to vocalize the vision that had fluttered inside his head. "I guess I always associate Thanksgiving with harvest, you know, a time to count your blessings like the Pilgrims did. So maybe bales of hay scattered around, a few pumpkins on top, a sheaf of wheat if you could find anyone to make it—that kind of thing."

"Sounds good," she said with a nod. "And easy. Sophie wants to have an evening meal outside so we'd need lights of some kind. I'd thought candles on the tables, but I suspect that's out because of the fire risk."

"There are lots of solar lanterns available. Or battery lights. You could even put some inside hollowed-out gourds and set those inside tipped-over bushel baskets. I've seen that done before." Wyatt felt silly throwing out these ideas about decorating, especially given the state of his ramshackle ranch. "Or you could string some lights in the trees. Maybe even leave them up for Christmas?"

"I love lights at Christmas." Ellie's eyes sparkled, her excitement obvious. "So, will you help me do it?"

"Uh, no. I mean, I can't. I, er, I'm busy with Cade," he stammered. Though he liked Ellie's enthusiasm, admired the way she threw herself into things, he pulled out the excuse he always used to escape involvement. He wasn't ever getting involved again anyway, so it was better to maintain his distance.

"Cade can sleep here while we work, as well as he can sleep at home." As Ellie called him out her face got a shrewd look. "In exchange for helping me with the decorating I could babysit for you once or twice. Gracie would love that."

This man would make a good daddy for us, Mommy.

Gracie's words reverberated in his head, and he knew he had to get out of this arrangement.

"I appreciate the offer, Ellie, but I don't think it would work." he said quickly and swallowed his coffee in a gulp. "I'd better get going. I've got chores to do at my ranch."

"You have a ranch?" Ellie's face had lost some of its excitement as she rose gracefully and walked with him toward Cade.

"It hardly deserves the term ranch, but I'm working on improving that," Wyatt told her, then grinned. "In my *spare* time."

Ellie smiled back before glancing at Cade. "He'll probably wake soon."

"Which is why I need to get home. He always wakes up hungry." Wyatt gently scooped the sleeping boy into his arms, relishing the baby powder smell of his son and the warm weight of him against his chest. "Thank you, Ellie. I appreciate all your help."

"You're welcome. It was my pleasure." She brushed one fingertip against Cade's cheek. "Bye, sweetie. I hope I see you again soon. You, too," she added, glancing at Wyatt.

He made a noncommittal response, feeling her gaze on him as he hurried to his truck. Funny how much he wanted to stay and enjoy her company. Ellie's warm personality, quick laughter and generous nature chased away the gloom and cares that had weighed him down for so long. Talking to Tanner and then sharing coffee with Ellie had, for a little while, brought Wyatt back into the adult world, a place where he didn't feel quite so incompetent.

As he drove home, Wyatt decided that today's

excursion proved that both he and Cade could benefit from more time among others. Right now he only had that on Sunday mornings when he took his son to church. But keeping an eighteen-month-old toddler amused and happy didn't allow much opportunity for Wyatt to hear the sermon, let alone interact with adults later. But at least the Sunday morning outing gave them both a break from their routine.

Maybe Ellie was right. Maybe there was a way Wyatt could manage to get more work done. After all, Cade slept in the afternoons. It was unlikely he'd know if his daddy was there or not, but even if he did, wouldn't Cade benefit from contact with more people? People like Ellie? Wyatt grinned. He had a hunch there wasn't anyone else quite like Ellie.

Wyatt pulled into his yard and carried a wakening Cade into the house, mindful that he was thinking an awful lot about Ellie Grant. Just as well he'd refused to help her with that Thanksgiving thing at Wranglers.

He admired her plucky spirit and generous outlook. But no way could he allow admiration to turn into anything else. Wyatt would not allow a relationship to grow between them. He failed at relationships. Failed his father and failed Taryn.

What he could not do was fail Cade.

* * *

The following day, after she'd finished work at Wranglers, Ellie bundled Gracie in the car and drove to Wyatt's ranch. All day she'd vacillated between compunction about invading his personal space when he'd made it clear he wanted nothing more to do with her and a silly female yen to hold Cade again.

Okay, *and* to see his good-looking father. It had been so nice to just talk to a male friend yesterday, one who wasn't her boss. She hadn't had that since Eddie had been part of her life.

"Hey, cut that out. Wyatt's a nice guy, but he's nothing to you," she reminded herself.

"What did you say, Mommy?" Gracie poked her head out from the book she'd been trying to read. A book about daddies, of course.

"Oh, just talking to myself, honey." Ellie gave herself a stern, though silent lecture about controlling her interest in the vet. Since the day they'd met Wyatt in the grocery store she'd repeatedly told her daughter that he could not be her father.

Well, neither can he be anyone special to you, Ellie Grant. But still, here you are driving onto his ranch on the faintest of pretexts...

"Is this where my new daddy lives?"

Her heart sinking, Ellie began, "Gracie, I've told you—"

"Look! Dogs, Mommy. Lots and lots of dogs." If there was one thing Gracie wanted almost as badly as she wanted a daddy, it was a dog. She clapped her hands in delight as Ellie parked near the house and several animals swarmed around the car, yapping excitedly.

"Don't open your door," she cautioned her daughter. "They might not be friendly. Wait."

When no one appeared, she tapped the horn. A moment later Wyatt poked his head around the corner of a dilapidated structure that might once have been a barn. He waved, disappeared for a moment, then began walking slowly toward them with Cade clinging to one hand, toddling along. As they came nearer, he gathered up the boy and shooed most of the dogs into a pen before shoving in a wooden stick to hold the loosened gate closed. But he left an adult German shepherd and a small puppy out. The shepherd went to lie down under a tree, but the puppy followed on Wyatt's heels to Ellie's car.

"Hey," he said when she rolled down her window. A question feathered across his face, but all he said was, "Welcome."

"Thanks." Seeing Gracie already had the door open and was exiting the car, Ellie followed her. "I'm sure you're busy, so I won't hold you up."

"No, it's good you came. I didn't realize the dogs had gotten out of the pen. That Irish setter is like a Houdini at escaping." He shook his head ruefully. "It's a good thing they're wearing collars for the electric fence."

"I think Gracie's already in love with this little one." Ellie smiled as a whirl of brown puppy raced circles around the little girl's sneakers, to her delight.

"Puppies. Their energy makes me feel old." Wyatt shook his head as the dog continued chasing his tail. "I was about to take a break. Want to join me for coffee?" He shifted Cade, who was sniffing and crying, to his other hip.

"Thank you. Oh, and I'm returning this." She lifted Cade's newly laundered blanket from the rear seat and held it out. "You left it behind yesterday."

He took the blanket, then shot her a confused look. "He has more than one blanket, Ellie. You didn't have to make a special trip. But thank you."

"I thought it might be his special *blankie*. Gracie would bawl for hours whenever hers went missing." Cade yelped and held out his arms to Ellie, jerking to be free of his father's hold. "He remembers me," she said with a chuckle, inordinately pleased. "May I take him?"

"Sure." Wyatt handed over his son, then led the way into his adobe ranch house.

"I see he's got a cold," she said. "They're the worst in little kids, aren't they?"

"Nope. They're the worst for adults. He was up most of last night with a fever." Wyatt shook his head. "He can't seem to settle much, poor little guy." He touched Cade's forehead. "Still cool."

"That's what we want. You have a lovely home." Ellie glanced around, trying not to appear too nosey but surprised at how show-homey it was beginning to look, even though parts were under construction. "The light is spectacular in here."

And everything is so perfectly planned, as if a professional designed this open concept layout.

"Thanks. One of the ladies from church asked to sit Cade last week. That's when I installed those French doors. They make a big difference."

Wyatt tossed his Stetson on a peg by the door, set the coffee brewer going, then glanced at Gracie who had flopped down on the floor and was cuddling the puppy she'd carried inside. "That's Mr. Fudge." He hunkered down beside her to scratch the dog's ears. "He's a chocolate lab."

"I like chocolate lots," Gracie told him. "But I really love dogs, 'specially baby dogs." She bent her head so her face was snuggled against Mr. Fudge's fur. "Mommy, can I have Mr. Fudge for my birthday?"

Ellie blushed as she remembered Gracie's request for a certain birthday gift of a daddy. But as she sat with Cade perched on her knee, her attention was diverted when the boy grabbed her beaded necklace and began chattering to himself in an unknown language. It felt so good to hold him, as right as it had yesterday.

Ellie knew that somehow she would have to rid herself of the yearning to cuddle another baby just as she needed to shed her lifelong dream to cherish a big family. Because it wasn't going to happen. So she tightened her grip on the little boy, determined to enjoy it while she could.

"Can I have this dog, Mommy?" Gracie pleaded. She lifted the squirming bundle in her arms and struggled to her feet, carrying the dog so Ellie could have a closer inspection. "See? Isn't he sweet?"

"He's very sweet, honey." Ellie touched her fingertips to the dog's ear, marveling at the silky skin. Aware of Wyatt's scrutiny she shook her head. "But I'm sorry, we can't get a dog. They don't allow them in the city complex where we live."

It was so hard to refuse her sweet daughter something as simple as a puppy. At Gracie's age Ellie's parents had given her a puppy of her own to cherish. If only…

Thankfully Wyatt intervened.

"I'm sorry, Gracie, but Mr. Fudge belongs to someone else. He's just here for a visit." He touched her bright head as he smiled. "His owners are coming to get him tomorrow morning."

"Well, I'm gonna pray we have to move into a new house so I can get a dog just like Mr. Fudge," Gracie announced. After shooting a stubborn look at Ellie she flopped down onto the floor and continued to play with the pup.

"Here, let me put Cade in his high chair." Wyatt scooped the little boy who'd begun to fuss from her arms.

"Oh, but I can hold—" Ellie's protest died with Wyatt's laughter.

"Believe me, you don't want to hold Cade when he's eating a cookie." He tied a bib around the boy and handed him a treat. "He makes a horrible mess."

I wouldn't mind. Ellie didn't say that. Instead she smiled politely, accepted the cup of coffee and the chocolate cookies he offered.

"All the dogs—your clinic is here at the ranch?" she asked.

"Yes, but mostly I just board animals here and go out to the calls." Wyatt shrugged. "I give shots here, if they're due. It keeps my name out there for prospective clients."

"So, out there, by the barn—" Ellie suddenly caught on. "You were working?"

"Trying to do a few much-needed repairs." Wyatt took two cookies for himself and bit into one. "Today wasn't optimum with Cade feeling off."

"How can you work with him nearby?" she blurted, unable to stop the question.

"I made him a tree swing." Wyatt chuckled when Cade dropped his cookie and began crowing with delight, arms swinging wildly. "Whoops, I said the word s-w-i-n-g. That's one he knows, and he loves riding in it." He held out another biscuit, and Cade soon forgot the topic. "I managed to get the hay changed and the stock fed during his sporadic rides. That's pretty good considering how he's feeling."

"Can I play with Mr. Fudge outside?" Gracie asked.

"Sure." Wyatt led her to the French doors, then glanced at Ellie. "The yard is fenced. Is it okay?"

"Yes, but don't go outside the fence, Gracie." She was thankful Wyatt didn't open the door until Gracie promised, doubly grateful when he slid the screen across so she could see and hear her daughter.

"I could—" Ellie began, but his phone interrupted her offer.

"Excuse me." Wyatt set down the washcloth he'd been wetting under the kitchen tap and answered the call. "No, that doesn't sound good," he agreed with a frown. He asked a few more questions, obviously about a sick animal, then said, "It could be contagious, but I can't tell for sure without seeing him, and I'm afraid I can't get away right now."

Ellie waved her hand to catch his attention.

"Hang on a moment, will you, Mark?" He put his hand over the receiver, a question on his face. "Yes?"

"Why don't you go do your job? I'll stay with Cade. I had nothing special planned for this evening anyway," she added, then thought how pathetic that sounded.

"I couldn't ask you to do that, Ellie." Wyatt shook his head.

"You're not asking. I'm offering. And I'd really enjoy spending some more time with this little guy." She dabbed Cade's cheek, and he sneezed. Seeing Wyatt's dubious look, she insisted. "Actually I was hoping you'd let us stay long enough to work on Gracie's school project."

"Oh?" he frowned.

"She's got to collect some pinecones for art class. I noticed you have tons scattered along your driveway. We could collect them and take Cade for a walk." She nodded when he just kept looking at her. "Go ahead. Take the call. It sounds serious."

"It could be." Wyatt had an obvious internal debate with himself, but it was equally obvious that he wanted to go. Finally, he nodded just once, then said into the phone, "Okay, Mark, I'm on my way."

Ellie smiled as he hung up. "Now, where's the stroller?"

"On the porch. You're sure about this?" He paused in the act of reaching for his hat. "You're not just trying to make me feel better or something?"

"Trust me, seeing your lovely ranch does not make me feel pity for you. Jealousy maybe. Look." She pointed outside to her daughter, suddenly a little too aware of the handsome vet standing beside her. Gracie ran around the yard with the puppy following. "I haven't heard her laugh like that for ages."

"Glad I could help." Wyatt slapped on his hat. "She must have her father's eyes," he said when the child looked up.

"No. Gracie has her mother's eyes." Ellie shook her head when he blinked in surprise. "I'll explain later. Go."

"I don't know how long I'll be." His worried gaze rested on Cade.

"We'll be here." She smiled when he looked at her. "I'm a nurse, Wyatt. I *can* take care of him."

"Of course. Thank you, Ellie," he said. He kissed Cade's head, then hurried out the door. A moment later his truck roared and he took off, a plume of red dust following.

"Mommy? Where did Cade's daddy go?" Gracie frowned, the puppy forgotten for the moment.

"Wyatt is a doctor for animals. He went to help them. He'll be back in a little while. Meanwhile, let's put the puppy in the pen and go for a walk to find those pinecones you need for school."

"Is Cade coming?" her daughter asked.

"Of course. Cade likes looking for pinecones," Ellie said as she went to take the child out of his high chair.

"How do you know?" Gracie's head tilted to one side, giving her the look of a curious bird. "Did his daddy tell you?"

"No. It's just one of those things mommies know."

As she picked up the baby and turned, her gaze fell on a huge portrait above the sofa. She walked over to study it.

Wyatt's wedding picture. He looked young and very happy, his dark eyes shining. The woman beside him was petite, her black hair upswept in a chic style. Even in the photo her love was obvious as her gaze locked with her new husband's. She wore a fancy, fluffy gown that looked very expensive. *Taryn & Wyatt* was engraved on a small silver plate along with a date.

Today's date.

Ellie gulped. Why had she come here today of all days, on their wedding anniversary? She was an interloper. Cade began protesting, and she glanced down, suddenly aware that this child was hers, Taryn's. She should be here comforting him, caring for him, sharing him with Wyatt.

"Come on, Gracie," she called suddenly. "Walk time."

Please, help me, Ellie prayed as she walked the children down the tree-covered lane, pausing here and there so Gracie could collect her cones. *I get carried away sometimes by my dream, by wanting what I can't have. Please, help me find a new dream, Your dream.*

Just before the spot where the lane joined the highway, Ellie paused and turned, the ranch spread out before her. It was a home for a family, but it could never be her home or her family. That dream had died the day she'd told her fiancé she would never be separated from her young child.

On that day Ellie had also realized that the dream she'd carried in her heart since childhood, a dream to be a mom to the kind of loving family her parents had given her and her sister, Karen, was just that—a dream. Her parents were gone, Karen was gone. All that was left of the Grant family was Ellie and Gracie.

And that had to be enough.

Chapter Three

Gracie has her mother's eyes.

With his animal patients well on the road to recovery, Wyatt's mind was free to puzzle over Ellie's words as he drove home. Wasn't *Ellie* Gracie's mother?

He pulled into his ranch, surprised by the warm glow he felt at seeing the house lights on as if to welcome him. He stood outside and paused a moment. In the twilight nothing looked amiss, as if this was a well-run hobby ranch instead of a work in progress. Still, Wyatt doubted his father would approve.

Inside the back door he inhaled the savory aroma of simmering beef. His stomach growled in response. Ellie walked toward him, a welcoming smile on her face.

"Hi. How'd things go?"

"Fine. The animal is recovering nicely." He

liked the way she'd bundled her silvery curls on the top of her head, leaving her pretty face and wide smile free for him to admire. "Everything okay here?"

"All quiet on the western front," she said. "Cade zonked out a while ago."

"I'll just go check on him." Wyatt washed first, then entered Cade's room, smiling at the sight of his boy curled up and snoring. His heart squeezed almost painfully tight as he smoothed a hand against Cade's dark head. "I love you, son," he murmured. He drew the blanket tighter, his heart welling with thankfulness that God had entrusted this small being to him. "Sleep well."

"I hope you don't mind that I put Gracie on the bed in your spare room," Ellie said when he returned to the kitchen. "I thought that way we wouldn't disturb her, and you can eat in peace."

"Very thoughtful, thanks. Speaking of eating… What is that tantalizing smell?"

"Oh, just some stew I made from that beef you had in the fridge." She lifted a dish from the oven. "I hope that's okay?"

"Yes, but—it's very kind of you to go to all this trouble." He licked his lips, slightly embarrassed when he realized Ellie was watching him. As her gaze held his he felt the intimacy in the room ramp up.

"I'm guessing you're hungry." Ellie's wide

smile brought a sparkle to her gray eyes like sunshine glinting off a granite rock.

"Starving." He took out a plate and Ellie filled it with beef, potatoes and green beans.

"I made some biscuits, too." She set them beside his plate.

"Biscuits?" He licked his lips. "I haven't had those for ages."

"Go ahead and eat. I'll make some tea," she said and immediately set the kettle to boil. "Do you cook?" She sat at the end of the breakfast bar, not far enough to break the friendly feeling but enough to give Wyatt some room.

"Oh, yes. My father was a firm believer that his kid should know how to fend for himself." He scooped up some stew. No way was he going to spoil this meal by talking about his unhappy childhood. But Ellie had other ideas.

"Your mom didn't mind you in her kitchen?" She rose as the kettle boiled.

"I never knew her." He smeared butter on the feathery light biscuits and watched it melt before taking a bite. "These are fantastic. Everything is. Thank you."

"I'm glad you're enjoying it." Ellie put the teapot and two cups on the counter. "Tanner told me your father was a well-known lawyer."

Which meant they'd been talking about him.

Wyatt didn't like that, but he didn't have time to dwell on it because Ellie was speaking again.

"You never had any desire to follow in his footsteps?"

"None. My first love has always been animals." No point in elaborating or discussing the many reasons why he hoped he'd never become like his father.

"I saw how much you care for animals."

Her comment shocked him. He stared at her, thinking that the flush of color on her cheeks suited her.

"I was walking Cade the other day when I saw you with that abused horse at Wranglers," she mumbled, her head tilted down. After a moment she looked directly at him. "He was filthy and mangy, and yet you touched him so gently, as if he was the most precious animal. You're a wonderful vet."

"Well, I try," he sputtered, a little surprised by the fervor of her words. Uncomfortable with her praise, he changed the subject. "Does that mean my son didn't settle as easily as you claimed?"

"He was restless, needed some fresh air." She shrugged. "He was fine."

"I see. Well, thank you for that. And for babysitting tonight and for supper."

"Oh." A furrow formed on her wide forehead

as she moved to the fridge and pulled out a bowl. "I almost forgot. Rice pudding?"

"My favorite." Wyatt spooned some onto his almost clean plate, slightly unnerved by how intimate it suddenly seemed in the dim room with two sleeping children next door. How was he going to let her know he wasn't interested in getting better acquainted? Although if he was honest with himself, he *was* curious about Ellie Grant.

He ate the pudding. "Delicious."

"Good." He saw her gaze swivel to focus on his wedding portrait. "Your wife was a very beautiful woman. Was she also a veterinarian?"

"Taryn?" Wyatt laughed as he scooped out a second helping of the pudding. "She was an interior designer. We were polar opposites. I'm country and she's—she was," he corrected automatically, "definitely city. The ranch was going to be our compromise. Only—" He bent his head.

"I'm so sorry for your loss, Wyatt." Somehow the generous compassion in Ellie's soft voice soothed his lingering hurt. "May I ask how she died?"

"A bunch of kids were joyriding and broadsided her car. The driver was underage and shouldn't even have been behind the wheel." As it always did, anger flared toward the teen. "He claimed it wasn't his fault, but it was." Wyatt stared at his hands, guilt welling inside. "It was also my fault."

Irritated that he hadn't yet found relief from the guilt of that awful day, Wyatt rose and loaded the dishwasher. He was fully aware that Ellie was watching every move with her all-seeing eyes, waiting. There was nothing else to do but explain. He poured two cups of tea and passed one to her.

"Taryn was out that night because of me. She should have been here, at home, with Cade. Instead she was running my errands." He stopped to clear the rasp from his throat. "My son will spend every Christmas without his mother because I didn't keep my promise." He didn't want to talk about the past anymore, so he turned the tables. "Why did you say Gracie has her mother's eyes?"

"Because she does." Ellie sipped her tea nonchalantly. She must have realized he didn't understand, because she suddenly set the cup down and smiled. "Sorry. I forget sometimes that people don't know our history. Biologically Gracie is my niece. My sister, Karen, was her mother. She died after Gracie was born and I adopted her a bit later."

So Ellie, too, carried pain. Wyatt sat down on a stool to listen, curious about the arrangement.

"Karen was married to Kurt. She was four months pregnant when he was killed in an accident at work. Kurt was in construction. He was on the job site one day trying to secure everything in a windstorm when a structure collapsed and killed him." Ellie sighed, her eyes tear-filled. "It was so hard for Karen to go on, but the pregnancy gave her courage. Then one day she phoned me in Chicago. She'd just found out she had brain cancer, and she'd decided to refuse all treatment in order to keep Gracie safe. I flew down to be with her. She died three months after Gracie's birth."

"Ellie, I'm so sorry." Wyatt reached out to touch her hand where it lay on the counter.

"So am I." Ellie glanced at his hand, then eased hers away. "Karen would have made an amazing mother. I'm just her stand-in. I promised her I'd do my best to be Gracie's mom but—" She shook her head as tears rolled down her cheeks. "I think I'm failing."

"How can you say that?" Uncomfortable with her tears but hearing the worry in her tone, he tried to reassure her. "Gracie's a great kid. I think you've done amazingly well with her."

"Then why isn't it enough? Why does she keep searching for a father?" Ellie asked, her voice breaking. "I love her so much. I've tried to give her everything she needs, but I can't give her a father!" She dashed away her tears, the gray irises darkening to slate. "There is no man in my life."

"Because?"

"Because that's the way it has to be." Ellie's cheeks bore dots of hot pink. "I was engaged, but that ended and I realized that God doesn't want me to have a romantic relationship. He wants me to focus on being Gracie's mom."

"Maybe it was the breakup with your fiancé that triggered Gracie's sudden interest in finding a daddy?" Wyatt privately thought her ex-fiancé must be an idiot to have let this woman go. "Maybe her hopes were dashed because she thought she was going to have a father like the other kids, and then she didn't get him."

"I don't think that's it," Ellie said slowly. "Because looking back, I realize Gracie never called Eddie Daddy. She always called him by name. When I explained we weren't getting married, she seemed okay with it. And she hasn't seemed upset about it since then. She was very excited about starting school. That's all she talked about."

"Well, maybe Eddie gave Gracie a sense of, I don't know, security? Maybe his male perspective is something she needs?" he said. "Is there someone else in your life who could take his place as a father figure?"

"But that's what I'm saying. Eddie wasn't a father figure in Gracie's world," Ellie protested.

"Maybe he was, and you didn't realize it." But even as he said it Wyatt found it hard to believe that Ellie could have missed something so important to her daughter. He'd seen just how caring and protective of Gracie she was. "Maybe there's someone you could ask to act as a male role model for her?"

"No." Ellie's voice was firm and unhesitating. "Tanner and Pastor Jeff are the only influential males in her life right now, and their lives are full with their own kids."

"Well, I'm no psychologist but..." Wyatt felt uncomfortable giving advice, but clearly Ellie wanted his opinion, and after all she'd done for him tonight, he could hardly throw up his hands and give up. "My guess is Gracie wants a closer bond with a man. Why? Maybe to show him off to her new school friends, maybe to have him take an interest in her that others haven't, or maybe she wants someone special that she can confide in."

"Why can't she confide in me?" Ellie said with a belligerent glare. "I am her mother."

"Did you tell your mother everything? Weren't there some times when you wanted to share with someone else?" In his own life Wyatt had never shared his hopes and dreams with his father.

He'd often wished he could, but knowing he'd be mocked had kept him silent.

"What does a little girl of five have to confide?" she asked.

"I have no clue." Wyatt felt like he was digging his way out of a quagmire. "But maybe Gracie thinks you wouldn't understand or that you'd try to dissuade her if she bared her heart. Or maybe she just needs perspective from another person."

"Which means I'm not enough." She looked so desolate that Wyatt hurried to reassure her.

"It doesn't mean that at all. It just means that she's growing up, expanding her world." He was speaking off the cuff, praying he said the right thing, because he had no clue how little girls' minds worked. "I don't think this is about you, Ellie. It's about her."

"But what do I do? She prays every night for God to give her a daddy. And now that she's met Cade, she's added a brother to her Christmas list." Ellie threw up her hands. "I can't make her understand," she wailed. "Sophie keeps telling me to pray about it and I am, but I'm not getting an answer and I need one because I don't know what I'm supposed to do."

"'If any man lack wisdom, let him ask of God.'" Wyatt shrugged. "I read that this morning. I guess you have to keep on God's case, asking Him to show you how to proceed."

"I guess." Ellie sighed. "Gracie's going to be heartbroken when a daddy doesn't appear at Christmas."

"Maybe I could talk to her a little, sound her out on what's behind her request." Wait a minute! What was he doing? He didn't want to get involved.

"I don't know if that's a good idea, Wyatt, though I thank you." Ellie nibbled on her lower lip. "Gracie's already fixated on you as the daddy of her dreams. Maybe you'd only make it worse, make her believe you really are moving into her life."

"I'd make sure she understands that I'm her friend, but I can't be her daddy." Wyatt had a lot more to say on the subject, including a warning to Ellie not to get the wrong impression about his offer. But he couldn't say it because the phone rang. "It's after hours. Let the machine pick up," he said when Ellie glanced from the phone to him.

"Wyatt, this is Jim Harder at the Triple T. I've been trying to reach you for days. You promised you'd do those inoculations this week, and I'm still waiting. I can't run a ranch like this. Call me tonight with a time to get it done in the next two days, or I'm looking for somebody else. I'd rather have you, but your hours are too erratic. I need a vet who gets here."

In the dead quiet of the room Wyatt stared at the answering machine, ashamed that Ellie had heard but frustrated because he knew he was about to lose his most understanding client. Cade was sick. How could Wyatt have left him with some nanny and walked away? But he also needed the work the Triple T offered. They had the biggest herd around. The income from that call alone could pay off some of Wyatt's bills.

"What are you going to do?" Ellie whispered.

"I don't know." He raked a hand through his hair, trying to come up with a plan. "I guess I could do the inoculations in bunches. It would take me a few days, but I could do it. But Cade's sick with this cold—" He shook his head. "I just don't know."

She studied him for several moments, saying nothing, dealing with her own private thoughts.

"We both need to pray for wisdom, I guess," she sighed after a few moments had passed. "Right now I have to get Gracie home. Thanks for letting me cry on your shoulder, Wyatt."

"I thought it was the other way around." He followed her into the bedroom, watching as she lifted a sleeping Gracie into her arms.

"She's too heavy for you," he said. "Let me take her." He didn't wait for Ellie's permission but instead scooped Gracie from her arms into his, smiling when the child's eyes fluttered open.

"Hi, Daddy," she murmured, then fell back asleep.

Wyatt met Ellie's gaze without saying anything. He followed Ellie out to her car and set Gracie in her car seat, then drew back so Ellie could fasten the seat belt, his mind working furiously.

"Listen," he blurted when she emerged from the car and had closed the door. "I have an idea. What if I spend some time with Gracie, just to clear up this daddy notion of hers?"

"In exchange for what?" Ellie's eyes searched his face.

"For you watching Cade for a few hours."

The look on her face told him she was about to reject his idea, so he rushed on. "I'll arrange for a nanny to come every morning as you suggested and handle office calls then. But I have to spend time working my ranch. If you could watch Cade for a couple of hours in the evening, I could get a lot done. Then maybe I'd be able to see more clients here."

"But the evenings, before bedtime, those are special daddy moments you shouldn't miss with Cade," she protested.

"Something has to give, Ellie." He hated admitting that. "I have to work *and* keep up our home."

"I know." She glanced down at Gracie, then back to him. Her lips tightened as if she wrestled with a decision, then she nodded. "What if I come over after I finish work at Wranglers Ranch? Gracie's finished school by then. We could stay with Cade, maybe make dinner, and then you'd be free to bathe him and put him to bed. Would that work?"

"It would." Wyatt slowly nodded while every brain cell in his head screamed a warning.

"I have just one condition," Ellie added, her voice deadly serious.

"Name it." Then he'd tell her his condition.

"You have to agree that this is simply an arrangement between friends and nothing more. I'm not looking for a father for Gracie or a relationship for myself. I need you to be clear on that, Wyatt. Strictly friends."

"Agreed," he said with a nod, relief swelling. "I don't want any romantic entanglements either. I want help with Cade, and I promise to do my best to help Gracie." He grinned at her and thrust out his hand. "Deal, *friend*?"

Ellie took her time but finally she shook hands with him. "Deal, friend."

Wyatt stood there, in the dimness of twilight, holding her soft hand, staring into her lovely face, and wondered if he was making a mistake.

"I have to go." Ellie pulled her hand free and

got into her car. She started it, then rolled down the window. "Beginning tomorrow?"

"Sounds good. We'll be here." He waved as she drove away until the twinkle of her red taillights had disappeared. Then he walked inside his house and checked on Cade.

Satisfied his son was sleeping peacefully Wyatt returned to the living room and let his gaze rest on his wedding photo. The same old lump of bitterness toward the youth who had caused Taryn's death burned inside his gut. If not for that kid his wife would be here and Wyatt's world would be fine.

Only it wasn't fine because he'd kept breaking his promises.

"That's not going to happen again," he told her, his shoulders going back. "I'm focusing on Cade first. Everything else comes second. I promi—"

Wyatt stopped himself from saying it. No more promises. Turning away he lifted a sleeping Mr. Fudge from his recliner and, after a quick trip outside, locked him in the laundry room to stay safe overnight.

As he walked past the kitchen to his office to work on his accounts, Wyatt caught a whiff of Ellie's spicy fragrance. He sat down at his desk thinking of her. She was a focused, determined woman, and she cared deeply for her daughter.

She would be an amazing caregiver for Cade, and Wyatt was certain she had no designs on him.

But what was he going to do about Gracie and her "daddy" quest?

Chapter Four

Wyatt's ranch was gorgeous.

While Gracie played with Cade in the sandbox, Ellie gazed at the ever changing horizon, mesmerized by the rosy hues of the November sunset above the craggy mountain peaks. For three evenings she'd watched this view and it was never the same.

Immersed in the display, she jumped when Wyatt asked, "Looking for something?"

"If I was, I found it. You have the most glorious sunset view I've ever seen." She tried to ignore the flutter of nerves his presence always brought.

"I do have that." He stood beside her, watching as the golden sun sank from view. "God's handiwork is pretty amazing."

"It is," she agreed, then snapped out of her daydream. "Are you finished already?" She checked her watch, surprised to find she'd been out here more than half an hour.

"I doubt I'll ever be finished on this place," Wyatt admitted in a dry tone. "But I'm finished for tonight." He lifted one shoulder and winced.

"Are you overdoing it?" Ellie asked as she shepherded the kids inside.

"No. I've just grown weak and out of shape since Cade came along." He grinned as he swung the boy in his arms and carried him inside to the bathroom. "Cleanup time. You, too, Gracie," he called over one shoulder.

"I'm coming." Gracie obediently trotted along behind him.

"And don't cheap out on the soap either," Wyatt warned. "I'm going to smell your hands when you're finished, and I only want to smell soap."

"Did your mommy used to smell your hands?"

Uh-oh. In the kitchen, Ellie froze at her daughter's question and the sudden silence that ensued.

"Supper's ready," she called, hoping to end Gracie's inquisitiveness and relieve Wyatt from the necessity of answering. To her surprise the three emerged with big grins. "What happened?" she asked in confusion.

"Cade splashed water all over the floor. We nearly floated away," Wyatt said as he set his son in his high chair. "And, no, Gracie. My mom didn't tell me that. Actually I didn't have a mom while I was growing up."

While Ellie set the serving dishes on the table she tried to decipher Wyatt's tone. She saw no distress on his handsome face.

"You didn't have a mom?" Gracie's eyes showed her shock. "How come? Did she die?"

"I don't know." Cade frowned as he fiddled with his cutlery. "Maybe. My father would never discuss her."

"So you didn't have a real fam'ly neither." Gracie frowned. "Just like me."

"Gracie, our family is real," Ellie began.

But Wyatt interrupted. "You and your mom are a family, Gracie. A very nice one, too." He smiled at her. "You don't know how blessed you are to have such a wonderful mommy."

"Yes, but—"

"Time to say grace," Ellie interrupted before her daughter got started on what was becoming her *daddy* theme song. "Hands together." She tucked her chin into her neck to hide her smile when Cade clasped his chubby hands together and closed his eyes.

"Thank You, God, for food, friends and family," Wyatt said. "Bless the hands that made this meal. Amen."

"Amen." When Ellie lifted her head she found him studying her in a curious way. She touched her fingers to her hair thinking she must have forgotten to comb it. "What are you staring at?" she asked, discomfited by his attention.

"You. Thank you very much for your help." Wyatt accepted the bowl she handed him, but his gaze returned to her. "I don't know how I'd have achieved so much without your help. I've got the kennels fully finished and the runs completely fenced now. Finally."

"That should help your business."

"It should," he agreed as he served Cade and Gracie. "But what I really want is to take in injured wild animals, treat them and give them a place to heal."

"Like Beth's rabbits?" Gracie asked with a full mouth. Catching her mother's warning look she gulped before continuing. "My teacher told us about some zoo animals that escaped. Are you gonna get lions here?"

"No lions." Wyatt chuckled. "I'm not sure what kind of animals I'll get, Gracie. So far that's just a dream."

"You have dreams?" she asked, surprised.

"Everybody has dreams, kiddo. Things we want to do or see or places we want to go, maybe people we want to meet. Even me." He smiled at her and took a bite of his food.

"I want you to be my daddy. That's my dream."

Ellie wanted to groan. How could she deal

with this? Nothing, not discouragement, explanations nor anything she'd tried so far, had worked.

"Gracie, honey, you are a very sweet girl," Wyatt said softly. "But I don't think I can be your daddy." He laid down his utensils so his complete focus was on her.

"You hafta. I've been praying so hard." Gracie frowned.

"I know you have. And I know God hears you. But sometimes God can't give us what we pray for, even though we really, really want it."

"Why not?" Gracie's bottom lip thrust out, and her face scrunched up in a frown.

Ellie waited for Wyatt to explain, content for now, to leave this to him. After all, that was their bargain, wasn't it?

"Because sometimes what we want isn't good for us," Wyatt said.

"Huh?" Gracie was clearly puzzled.

"Well, think of it this way. God is a father, right? Our Father."

"Yeah." Gracie nodded.

"I'm a father, too. I'm Cade's father." He shot his son such a proud look that Ellie caught her breath at the love shining in his eyes.

"When he gets a little older and starts asking me for things, do you think I should give him everything he asks for?"

"I dunno," Gracie replied. But Ellie could see that Wyatt's message was getting through as her daughter suddenly concentrated on her meal.

"Sure you do." Wyatt handed Cade half a roll. "If he asked for something to eat, do you think I'd give him that?"

"Yes." Gracie nodded without hesitation.

"What if Cade asked me for candy?" Wyatt said next.

"Candy tastes good. Cade likes choc'lat." Gracie grinned at the little boy. "Me, too."

"So it'd be okay if I gave Cade chocolate every time he asked for it?" Now Wyatt nonchalantly chewed on his salad.

Ellie wanted to cheer at his strategy. First her daughter nodded vigorously, then paused.

"Maybe not every time," Gracie said finally.

"But why not? You said Cade likes chocolate, and eating it makes him happy. I sure want my boy to be happy."

"He'll get sick." Gracie made a face. "I ate too much candy at Melissa's birthday, and I got a tummy ache. It hurt a lot."

"And I don't want Cade to get sick. I sure don't want him to hurt." Wyatt paused and held her gaze to make sure she heard him. "So sometimes when Cade asks me for candy I will have to say no. Because that's what's best for him, and as his daddy, I always want what's best for my child. Because I love him. Right, Gracie?"

Ellie's glance met Wyatt's. He smiled encouragement, but she couldn't return his smile. This was too important. Gracie *had* to understand that he was not going to be her father. That no one was.

"So even if Cade keeps asking me over and over, I can't give him what he wants." Wyatt's tone was so tender as he added, "Because I love him."

"But I didn't ask God for candy," Gracie protested. "I want a daddy. You."

"I know, honey. But it works the very same way." Wyatt leaned in so he could look directly into her eyes. "Getting you a daddy—that's up to God. God's your Father, and He loves you very much. If He wants you to have a daddy, then when He's ready, He'll make it happen. But *you* can't make it happen, Gracie."

Ellie held her breath, waiting to see how Gracie accepted this. Her daughter went on eating, and Ellie wondered if she'd finally give up her daddy quest.

Then Gracie looked up at Wyatt. "You mean I shouldn't pray for a daddy. But my Sunday school teacher said we should always tell God what we want."

"You should always pray, Gracie." Wyatt's

face was very serious. "Even if your mom can't give you every single thing you ask for, you talk to her about other things, don't you?"

"Yeah." Gracie nodded.

"Well, that's how it is with God. We tell Him all about what's in our hearts, and He listens because He loves us." Wyatt lifted his gaze to Ellie as if asking her what else he could say.

Ellie scrambled for something to add, but Gracie preempted her.

"Pastor Jeff was talking at church one time about a woman in the Bible who kept asking Jesus to make her better even after He didn't do it right away." She focused on Wyatt with intensity. "Pastor Jeff said Jesus healed her, and maybe it was 'cause He just wanted her to stop asking. So that's what I'm gonna do. I'm gonna keep asking God for you for my daddy."

Ellie sagged in her seat. She'd been so sure—

"Maybe He'll do it just to stop me askin'," she said thoughtfully and finished the food left on her plate. "Are we havin' dessert?"

Aware that Wyatt had pushed away his unfinished plate after a resigned sigh, Ellie rose and served dishes of pecan pie.

"I bought it from a roadside market on the way over here. I hope they make a good pie," she said.

"They certainly do," Wyatt said after he'd

tasted a bite. "Thank you very much, Ellie. I haven't had pie in a long time."

"I have ice cream for Cade," she said. A moment later she handed the little boy a cone which he grabbed and bit into. A surprised look filled his face as the cold hit, then he squealed, laughed and took another bite.

"I guess that means he likes it." Wyatt grinned at her, and for the life of her Ellie couldn't stop herself from grinning back at him like some kind of coconspirator. But wasn't that exactly what they were?

"I guess it's back to washing hands and faces," Wyatt said when everyone had finished their dessert. "Come on, Gracie, you, too. You can't get in your mom's car looking like that."

"Why not?" she asked as she followed him to clean up.

"What if a policeman stopped you?" Wyatt's booming laugh filled the house. "He'd have to give your mom a ticket for having a daughter with such a grubby face."

He was so good with Gracie that it was a shame he couldn't be— No!

Ellie stopped that thought dead in the water. That was ridiculous. She didn't want any romantic entanglements. She had all she could do working at Wranglers, babysitting Cade and caring for Gracie.

But as Wyatt waved her off and she drove home, Ellie couldn't help the silly little picture that filled her mind of a family having a picnic around Wyatt's big fire pit.

"Not your family," she chided her wayward brain.

"Are you talking to yourself again, Mommy?" Gracie asked.

"I guess so."

"If you're talking to you, who am I gonna talk to?" Gracie crossed her arms over her chest with a sigh. "I guess I hafta talk to God some more about gettin' me my daddy."

"Me, too," Ellie agreed gloomily under her breath.

She'd also have to talk to Wyatt again. Because nice as his try was, it hadn't deterred Gracie in the least.

Wyatt wasn't exactly sure what a pre-Thanksgiving-evening get-together at Wranglers Ranch included, but he'd come because Tanner had asked him to and because he wanted the company. Somehow he'd never imagined there would be people rushing around the place like whirling dervishes.

He walked with his son at his side to where Ellie was balancing on a stump, holding up a rope for Tanner who had climbed a eucalyptus tree and was clinging to it with one arm stretched out, trying to reach the rope to tie it on the branch.

"What's going on?" Wyatt asked, then glanced down when something tugged his pant leg.

"We're helpin' Mommy get ready for the giving thanks day decoratin'." Gracie lifted a paper pumpkin for him to admire. "Can you please hang this up, Daddy?"

"Gracie Grant," her mother warned, cheeks flushed bright pink as she teetered on her perch. "We've talked about this. You may call him Wyatt or Mr. Wright. You may not call him Daddy."

"But he is going to be—"

"Not another word or you'll be having a time-out while everyone else celebrates tomorrow." Ellie glared at her daughter until Gracie sighed and nodded. Ellie's smile reappeared. "Good. And it's called Thanksgiving."

"But that's what I said, isn't it?" Gracie looked so confused Wyatt's heart melted.

"It's a really nice pumpkin," he said to cheer her up.

Her face came alive. "Thank you, Da—Mr.— um, thanks."

"Hand me your pumpkin, honey." Ellie sent Wyatt a warning look that made him stifle his amusement. "Tanner will hang it up for you."

Once hung, the orange ball fluttered in the breeze. "Doesn't it look nice up there?"

"Yup." Gracie dashed off to find Beth.

"See why I'm no good at decorating? I did not know pumpkins hung from trees," Wyatt said, tongue in cheek. Cade flopped onto his bottom to play with his ball, so he held out a hand. "Get down from there, Ellie. Tanner and I will take care of the rest of the hanging."

"It's only a little stump," Ellie protested, clasping his hand for support as she descended.

"Who'd be left to treat the sick and injured if the nurse got hurt?" Wyatt thought how perfectly her hand fit in his, until she pulled it away.

"I was fine, you know." She scooped Cade from the ground and pressed a kiss against his cheek. "But I won't argue if it means I get to hold this little guy."

Wyatt spent the next hour following her decorating directions, and he didn't mind helping one bit because Ellie made everything fun. He hauled bales and arranged them to Ellie's specifications. Moses brought a bunch of old lanterns, buckets and other antiques, and under Ellie's supervision Wyatt set up displays. That turned into a fiasco so Ellie took over. Then Sophie produced six boxes of tiny white twinkle lights which Wyatt and Tanner strung above the patio.

When the last table centerpiece of pinecones,

cinnamon sticks and battery-operated candles were in place Tanner called a halt.

"That's enough. Remember, we'll have to take it all down tomorrow," he groaned, rubbing his back.

"Not the lights. They can stay until after Christmas." Ellie's smile made Wyatt feel like he was a part of the Wranglers' group. "Thank you, everyone. I think the kids will love it."

"Time for a snack," Sophie called. They all gathered around the outdoor kitchen to enjoy mugs of cocoa and fudge brownies.

"Your reputation is well deserved," Wyatt praised Sophie when he took his third treat. "These are delicious."

"Oh, I didn't make those. Ellie did." Sophie grinned at her friend. "And I agree. I'm thinking of offering her a second job as baker for my catering business."

"Maybe you could teach me to make them," he said to Ellie.

"Sure. They're simple. It's my sister Karen's recipe. She was a chocoholic." For a moment a shadow passed over her eyes, then she brightened and tickled Cade under the chin. "Did you get any in your mouth?" she teased, wiping his chocolate-covered cheeks with a napkin.

"I did." Gracie grinned, showing brown-stained teeth. "Can me and Beth take some to the rabbits?"

Four adults all said "No!" at the same time.

Wyatt squatted down to Gracie's level. "Chocolate is very bad for the rabbits' tummies, Gracie. It makes them really sick."

"Dogs, too?" she asked with a frown glancing at Sophie and Tanner's dog. One hand poked out from behind her back. On her palm lay a mashed square of brownie. "I was gonna give this to Sheba."

"Dogs, too," he said with a firm nod.

"Oh." Gracie looked at the mashed dessert for a moment, then dumped it into his hand. "Okay." She bounded away, calling Beth and Davy to come play catch.

"Oh, dear." Ellie's eyes twinkled with amusement. She giggled at the face Wyatt made when he couldn't dislodge the sticky mess into a napkin. "Since you have to go inside to wash, you might as well take Cade." She lifted the boy and handed him over to Wyatt.

"What? No wipes to clean us up?" he teased, enjoying the way her face suffused with color.

"I don't have my bag handy," she said, glaring at him. "And you'd better get going before he plasters your shirt with chocolate."

"More laundry." With a sigh Wyatt headed inside for wash-up duty.

When he emerged the entire group was gathered around the glowing fire pit on the patio. Only the twinkle lights and the flickering flames provided light on the patio, just enough for Wyatt to see an empty space beside Ellie. He took it and cuddled an already dozing Cade on his knee, warmed by the sweet smile she gave him when he brushed against her shoulder.

That was the thing about Ellie. She always made you feel better, and it didn't have a thing to do with her nursing skills. She simply radiated warmth and inclusion, and she went overboard trying to make sure no one was left out. Hence the surfeit of decorations, an exuberant, over-the-top gesture meant purely to give joy to kids who'd visit the ranch for Thanksgiving.

"We always have stories around the campfire," Beth explained to Gracie. "What's the story tonight?" she asked Tanner.

"It's about giving thanks," he said and began. "A very long time ago there were ten lepers. Leprosy is a very bad disease," he explained to the children. "It's painful and it's contagious."

"That means other people could get it from them," Ellie interjected, then shrugged when Wyatt grinned at her. "I can't help it. I'm a nurse. I like medical clarity."

Tanner grinned at her, then paused until he

had everyone's attention again. "So the people who had leprosy had to stay away from everyone, even their families, so they didn't pass it on to others." Tanner's voice was low, and the kids had to lean in to hear. "Whenever the lepers walked past, someone would yell 'Unclean,' so that everyone would step out of the way, so that they didn't catch it, too."

"What a lonely way to live." Ellie's murmur was so low Wyatt doubted anyone else heard. "The pain of leprosy would be as bad as losing your loved ones."

Wyatt knew from the emotion in her voice that she'd gone through those hard lonely times herself after her sister's death. Maybe she still was. Was that why Ellie worked so hard at everything she took on? Because she was trying to stay busy? Just as he was?

"So when these ten lepers heard about Jesus healing people, they decided they wanted to see Him. They didn't have medicine, so there was no other way for them to get well." Tanner spoke slowly, ensuring the enraptured children hung on every word. "So they asked Jesus to heal them. And He did."

"He made them all better. That was good," Beth said.

"Yes, it was." Tanner's smile lingered on his

adopted daughter a moment before his voice dropped to a serious note. "There was just one thing wrong. Only one of the lepers came back to say thank you. Only one out of ten that Jesus made better." Tanner let them think about that for a minute. "That's why Thanksgiving Day is so important. Because it reminds us to be thankful for what God has given us. What are you thankful for?"

"Skateboards," Davy called out.

"Bunnies," was Beth's answer.

And so it went around the group. Until it came to Wyatt. He looked down at Cade, sleeping peacefully in his arms. Too often he forgot to count his blessings.

"Him," he whispered through the lump in his throat. He lifted his head and glanced around. "And all of you."

"That's what I'm thankful for, too," Ellie said softly. "Gracie, Wranglers Ranch and friends. You've all made a tremendous difference in my life this past year."

The only person who hadn't spoken was Gracie. Wyatt thought she'd fallen asleep until Tanner asked, "What are you thankful for, Gracie?"

"I can't say it." She peeked through her lashes at her mother, then quickly looked away.

"Sure you can. Tell us, sweetheart," Ellie encouraged.

Wyatt didn't think she'd answer. Then all at once Gracie inhaled and spoke, a hint of defiance in her voice.

"I'm thankful that God is going to give me my daddy, even if you don't think so," she said with a glare at her mother. Then, bursting into tears, she jumped up and ran into the darkness.

"Gracie!" Ellie rose, but noting the tight angry look in her eyes Wyatt decided to intervene.

"Here." He shifted Cade into her arms. "Let me go. I'll talk to her."

"But I'm her mother—" When Ellie hesitated Wyatt touched her arm.

"You're upset and so is she. Let me go." He leaned forward to whisper in her ear. "That's our deal, right? For me to help her with this fixation."

The sweet scent of jasmine filled his nostrils. In a flash that fragrance of Ellie's perfume started a video in his brain of a hundred different images of her caring for others. Now it was his turn to help her.

"Please?" he murmured. Her gaze met his, flames flickering in their depths until finally she nodded.

"Just be—"

"I'll be very gentle with her," he promised and squeezed her hand.

"I know you will. It's just—she's all I have." She squeezed back, smiled, then released his fingers.

Wyatt walked away, knowing he had to do his best. For Ellie. Because she always did her best for others. So he found Gracie, in the bunny pen of course, and let her cry on his shoulder as she poured out her deepest desire.

"I want you for my daddy," she wailed through her tears. Hearing the longing in her words was like having her little hand reach in and squeeze his heart.

Wyatt had no idea how to help her, so he simply held her while he silently prayed for wisdom. When she'd finally calmed down, he took a deep breath and began to speak.

"Gracie, sweetie, hush and listen to me now." She sniffed and rubbed her eyes but paid attention. "Your mom and I have tried to tell you that I can't be your daddy. But you won't stop thinking about it all the time. It's like you have a sore on your finger, and you won't let it heal. That's what is hurting you. I think you need to forget about having a daddy, for a little while."

"But—"

Wyatt put a finger across her lips and shook his head. Finally, Gracie slumped, signaling her willingness to listen. In the gentlest words possible he used every argument he could come up with, short of telling her he had no intention of taking on the care and upbringing of another child.

He hoped he'd finally convinced her to let go of him as her daddy. In fact, he was certain he had because he asked her three times if she understood, and each time Gracie nodded soberly.

"Okay, then. Good." Wyatt wondered why he didn't feel relief that she wouldn't be counting on him anymore, but he brushed away the wayward thought and hugged her as Ellie called her daughter's name. "We're coming," he replied, then turned back to Gracie. "Is everything good with us?"

"Uh-huh." She swung his hand as they walked over the path. "I heard what you said."

"And?" He saw Ellie coming but wanted Gracie's compliance before her mother arrived. "What do you think?"

"I think God can do lots of things, 'specially things adults don't believe." She let go of his hand and smiled. "You don't have to worry. God *is* gonna make you my daddy. I just gotta wait." Then she skipped past her mother and onto the patio where she announced, "I'm thankful God answers my prayers."

Ellie glared at him.

"What on earth did you say to my daughter, Wyatt?" she demanded in a whisper. "I don't want her believing that you are going to be her father."

"Neither do I," he sputtered indignantly. "I tried to tell her that, but she just won't listen." Then the funny side of it hit him, and he burst out laughing. "You have to admire her faith, though. It's a lot stronger than mine."

"That's your response to this…catastrophe?" Ellie handed him Cade, her eyes steely as she stood under the twinkle lights. "I'm not sure this agreement of ours is working out, not if it's adding to Gracie's hope that we are somehow going to become a family."

He sobered immediately. "What are you saying, Ellie?"

"I'm saying that I don't think I should come over and stay with Cade anymore." She gazed mournfully at his sleeping child, then sighed. "I'm sorry."

Stunned by the loss he felt at just the thought of not seeing Ellie each afternoon, Wyatt reeled.

"I have to do what's best for Gracie," Ellie said. "She's my primary concern."

"Of course, but—" Wyatt touched her arm. "I don't think you not caring for Cade is going to change her mind, Ellie. In fact, I think the only way to dissuade her is to prove to her that we are friends, but that we're *only* friends. When she sees there's nothing more, she'll give up."

"Are you sure?" she asked dubiously.

Wyatt wasn't sure at all. But the past few weeks Ellie had been coming to his ranch had been some of the best he'd had in the past year. He felt happier knowing he was accomplishing some of his postponed goals, practicing his vocation, all the while knowing Cade was in good hands. Lately, thanks to Ellie, both of the Wright men were happier. Wyatt had even managed to brood less about Ted, the boy who'd killed Taryn.

"Don't you like caring for Cade?" he asked, appealing to her motherly side.

"You know I do. But Gracie—" She frowned, watching as her daughter and Beth played hopscotch on the patio.

"I have an idea about Gracie," he said. "Something that just might change her mind about having me for a father."

"What is it?"

"Wait and see." Cade shifted, and Wyatt checked his watch. "I better get home. See you tomorrow."

As he walked away Ellie called his name.

Wyatt paused, turned and studied her face.

"Don't hurt her," she begged.

"Letting go of her dream might hurt Gracie for a little while, Ellie." How lovely she looked in the cascade of light from overhead. "But I promise I won't deliberately do anything to harm her." *Promise? Another promise?*

"Okay." After a very long pause she nodded. "Partner."

Wyatt left, wondering as he drove home why he suddenly felt disheartened. He certainly didn't want more than friendship with Ellie.

Or did he?

Chapter Five

"Ellie Grant, you're like a cat on a hot tin roof." Sophie edged around her to set down a pan of rolls fresh from the oven. "Waiting for Wyatt?" she asked, tongue in cheek.

"Sort of." Ellie blushed at the insinuation on her friend's face. "Not like that. I've told you before that I'm not interested in a romantic relationship."

"Yes, you did *say* that." Sophie slid two more pans into the oven. "But whenever Wyatt's around, you light up like a Christmas tree." She frowned. "Speaking of which, I wanted to ask Tanner to get that big spruce by the entry gates decorated before our dinner today."

"Sophie." Ellie snapped her fingers to get her friend's attention. "Wyatt and I are not having a romantic relationship. We're simply helping with each other's children."

"Right." Sophie tried to hide her smile, but Ellie saw it nonetheless.

"It's true," she insisted, ignoring the curious looks of Sophie's two helpers. "But I am anxious to see him today because he said last night that he has a plan to get Gracie to change her mind about him as her father. I want to know what his plan is."

"Of course. And that's why you keep checking the clock every ten seconds." Sophie chuckled. "Well, check no more, my friend. I believe that's his truck rumbling into view."

"Really?" Ellie raced to the window and peered outside. "He's here?"

"Yup. I can sure see how it's all about Gracie." Sophie's amused grin stretched from ear to ear. "Now, scoot! Go talk to him, so we can get some work done in here," she ordered.

"Yes, ma'am." Ellie scooted out the door and across the yard, feeling like a giddy schoolgirl as she waited for Wyatt to park his truck. "Hi," she said when he stepped down.

"Hi, yourself." His lazy smile did funny things to her stomach where butterflies were already dancing a jig. "How's it going?"

"Well, since I was just shooed out of the kitchen I thought I'd let Cade entertain me." She had to move, to break free of this odd rush of nerves, so she walked around the truck to the other side and released the little boy from his car seat. "Hey, you," she said, loving the way he reached for her.

"Is there something I should help with before the kids arrive?" Wyatt grabbed Cade's bag from the truck.

"I'm not sure. But be warned that if you go into the kitchen, Sophie's going to ask you to decorate that big tree by the gate." She laughed when he panned a look of terror. "It wouldn't be that bad."

"We all know how useless I am at decorating. We hardly need more proof after last night."

"Let's just say that you're better at pretty much anything to do with animals." She tried to hide her amusement but couldn't at the memory of him arranging gourds and pumpkins that would not stay put. "You have to admit it was funny how they kept rolling all over."

"Hilarious." He leaned back on the fence rail to study her. "You look pretty. Relaxed, ready to handle whatever crops up."

"Well, thank you." She felt inordinately pleased by the compliment. "What could crop up?"

"I have no idea." He winked. "That's what scares me."

"Let's go find Tanner and see what he'd like us to help with." More disturbed by this man than she wanted to admit to herself, Ellie headed toward the tack room with Cade walking beside her.

"Where's Gracie?" Wyatt ambled on her other side, his Stetson pushed to the back of his head.

"With Beth and the bunnies, of course." She wanted to contain her curiosity, but the question had been bugging her all night. "What's your plan, Wyatt?"

"Watch." He shot her a grin, then moved nearer the bunny pen and peered inside. "Hey, girls," he called. "How're those baby bunnies doing?"

"Good. Want to come see them?" Beth called. Gracie remained silent, watching.

"Sure." Wyatt wore a poker face as he looked at Ellie. "You may want to go back to the house or busy yourself with something else. I have work to do here." He took Cade and handed her his bag. "And this guy's going to help me."

"But—" She stared at him, unable to believe he was asking her to leave.

"See you later, Ellie," Wyatt said loudly, waving before he opened the gate and went inside the rabbit pen.

Frustrated that she wasn't to be included, Ellie considered going to check her supplies.

Only she couldn't leave. So instead she found a spot by the side of an outbuilding where she could surreptitiously watch Wyatt, Gracie and

Cade without being seen. Beth left when Tanner called her away, so Ellie leaned in, trying to hear what Wyatt was saying to her daughter; but she was unable to catch it because of the noise of arriving guests. Minutes later Wyatt was leading Gracie and Cade out of the paddock, so apparently their "talk" was over. Not wanting to be caught, Ellie took her time returning to the house.

"Where've you been?" Wyatt asked when she stepped onto the patio. He looked hot and tired and more frustrated than she'd ever seen him.

"Is something wrong? Where's Gracie?" Ellie didn't like the look of the red spots in his cheeks or the way his eyes narrowed to mere slits. "Wyatt, is there something I should know?"

"Not really. Oh, wait. There is one little thing," he said sarcastically. "Your daughter is now telling every single kid at Wranglers Ranch that I've been showing her how to babysit Cade so that when we get married—" He shook his head in disgust, then dragged a hand through his hair.

"When we what?" She could only gape at him.

"When we get *married* so I can be her *daddy*, and after we *have more kids*," he enunciated clearly and precisely, "then she'll be able to look after them. Because that's what *big sisters do*." His groan sounded heartfelt. "How could a plan go so wrong?"

Words failed Ellie. The only thing she could do was sit down.

And pray he was joking.

For the first time all day Wyatt finally relaxed. With a little help here and there, the animals on Wranglers Ranch had survived an afternoon among tons of kids. He'd done his job. Now, seated beside Ellie with Gracie on her far side, at a table laden with delicious food, surrounded by laughing, happy kids, he exhaled the frustrations of the day and closed his eyes as Tanner said grace.

"Father, we thank You for Your blessings to us, for health, for friends and most of all for sending Your son to be our Savior. We can never repay the debt we owe You. All we can say is thank You. So thank You, Father. Amen."

Friends. Was that what he'd been missing since Taryn's death? People who cheered you and supported you. *And forgave you.*

"Rolls?" Ellie handed him the basket without meeting his gaze.

"Thanks." Wyatt took two and passed on the rest. And so it went. Ellie passed him the potatoes, the gravy, the stuffing and the turkey, all without comment. Apparently she wasn't yet over her anger. "I didn't do it on purpose," he finally whispered in her ear, liking the feel of the silken strands against his skin. "It just didn't go right, that's all."

"Really?" He'd never realized gray eyes could look so glacial. *"It didn't go right?"* Her voice brimmed with mockery.

"Ellie, I—"

She turned her shoulder and began speaking to the boy across the table from her, her face suddenly bright and animated, though her body language screamed anger.

"Fine. I'll talk to you." Frustrated, he turned to his son, but Cade's interest was captured by a young girl who tickled and teased him as she helped him eat his dinner. Wyatt had never felt so alone among so many people.

Every time he looked at Ellie, she made an excuse to leave the table. She laughed, she joked, and she constantly smiled—at everyone but him. As Wyatt fed Cade the last bite of his pumpkin pie, he decided it was time to go home.

"Can you take a look at something before you go?" Tanner asked when he'd thanked his host.

"If you need me to." Wyatt wished he'd used the confusion of clearing the tables and kids departing to leave. He felt discouraged and defeated, and he did not want to run into Gracie or her mother again.

"Let's leave Cade with Ellie," Tanner suggested, but Wyatt balked.

"She's busy," he refused quickly. "I'd rather take him along."

"Okay." Tanner gave him a long look, then led the way toward the east paddock where several mares were grazing. "See the chestnut mare over there?"

"It's pretty dark out here, Tanner." Wyatt squinted, trying to figure out what was so important. "And I'm too far away to tell much anyway. It would be better if I come back tomorrow to examine her."

"Oh, I don't think you need to worry about her. I just wanted to show her off." A funny little smile tipped the side of his mouth. "She's pregnant. And so are we."

"We?" It took a moment for Wyatt to get it. "You mean you and Sophie? Wow. Congratulations." He held out his hand and shook Tanner's. "That's great, man."

"Yeah, it is. I can hardly wait to see my son or daughter." Tanner's face shone in the moonlight. "That mare's just one more reason why I'd like to have you at Wranglers full-time, Wyatt. So you could watch her progress, not just check on her now and then."

"I can't, Tanner. I'd like to, but I'm not ready to give up on trying to build my practice," Wyatt refused. "Not yet anyway."

"It's not going well?" The rancher led him

to an old wrought-iron bench, and they sat together on it. Thankfully, Cade had fallen asleep in his arms.

"I thought I was making progress, thanks to Ellie helping out with Cade." Wyatt pressed his lips together. "Her being there really made a difference. I could get things done, spend a little longer on a call if I had to without worrying about Cade."

"So, what's the problem?" Tanner frowned.

"Gracie." Wyatt wasn't exactly sure where to begin, so he just spilled his guts. "I had this idea that if Gracie knew that it isn't all a bed of roses to have a little brother, then maybe she'd rethink this idea of me being her father."

"You thought you could talk Gracie out of her daddy goal?" Tanner huffed a laugh, then apologized. "Sorry. It's just that the strength of that child's faith in God answering her prayers often makes me feel like a wimp."

"I know the feeling." Wyatt sighed. "Anyway I messed up."

"I heard a rumor that you and Ellie are getting married and having kids." Tanner was trying not to laugh.

"Obviously, Gracie didn't quite get my point," Wyatt mumbled, utterly embarrassed. "And Ellie's really mad. She isn't going to come out to my place anymore. She thinks that might help get Gracie's mind off—uh, me."

"You think she's right?" Tanner studied Wyatt's face, then nodded. "Me, neither. That little girl isn't going to let go of her dream so easily." He paused before softly asking, "You don't want to make that sweet child's deepest longing come true?"

"No." Wyatt glared at Tanner. "My wife's dead because I didn't keep my promise to her. Now I have a kid to raise on my own. That's all I can handle, Tanner. I'm sure not making any more promises that I'll end up breaking. Besides, Ellie and I are just—"

He didn't finish that sentence, because it wasn't true anymore. He was pretty sure they weren't friends any longer.

"Ellie will come around. You'll see," Tanner insisted. "She's just frustrated at not being able to control Gracie."

"She can join the club." Wyatt rose. "I need to get this guy home. Thanks a lot for the party. It was fun."

"I'm sorry we had to put you to work, but I sure am grateful you spotted Abigail's lame leg. That splint you put on her should help." Tanner walked with him toward his truck, waited while he buckled Cade into his seat. "If you need help, call me, Wyatt. And send me a bill for today. You deserve to be paid for all your help."

"It was no trouble, and I did get two pieces of pie." He shook hands with the chuckling rancher then drove away.

Just before he turned the corner he saw Ellie standing beside the big tree she'd said Sophie wanted to have decorated before Christmas. She didn't wave. In fact, she made no indication that she'd even noticed him. But Wyatt knew she had. Just as he always noticed when she was near.

Maybe it's better if she stays away. Maybe I'm getting too interested in her and Gracie.

Wyatt figured the next little while was going to be lonely until he got used to not seeing Ellie's smiling face every day. He'd have to pray harder that God would send him someone to help with Cade because one thing hadn't changed. He still hadn't fulfilled the promise to his father to make his veterinary practice the best in the city.

Thing was, Wyatt wasn't sure he even wanted to.

Ellie stood in the little log cabin that now served as her nursing station, unabashedly listening to Tanner talking on his phone outside.

"I'm going over to Wyatt's, Sophie. I haven't seen him for two days, and he doesn't answer his phone. I'm wondering if something's wrong.

He was pretty down when he left Thanksgiving night."

The words caused a rush of shame so intense that she missed the rest of the conversation. She desperately regretted her chilly attitude to Wyatt that night. He'd only been trying to help her, after all. It was just that she'd been so utterly embarrassed by Gracie's declarations and certain they wouldn't have happened if he hadn't caused it.

Totally unfair. She realized that now. Gracie was going to believe what Gracie believed until someone other than her mother or Wyatt proved her wrong. But it was hard to eat crow, to apologize to him and take back her words about watching Cade.

She stepped outside the door and hailed Tanner.

"I heard you say you're on your way to Wyatt's. If there's anything I can do, will you let me know?" She saw her boss's eyebrow arch in surprise, but he simply nodded. "Thanks."

She watched him drive away, a prayer in her heart for the man she couldn't get out of her mind. She'd treated Wyatt shabbily. He'd no doubt been just as embarrassed as she.

"I goofed, God," she mumbled as she dusted the office while waiting for Gracie to arrive on the bus. "And I should have known better. I'm not *that* new a Christian."

Gracie's appearance and jubilant explanation about her day at school took center stage, and for a few moments Ellie forgot to worry. Until her phone rang and Tanner said, "Ellie, can you get over here right away? Wyatt and Cade are both sick as dogs. I need you to check them out while I see to his stock."

"On my way." She ushered Gracie into her car seat as she explained where they were going.

Once they were at the Wright house, Cade's wails demanded her attention. So did Wyatt. He sat on a kitchen chair, haggard, pale and disheveled.

"Thanks for coming," he rasped. "I don't know what's wrong with him. Since I can't seem to stand without getting dizzy I'm scared to pick him up."

"Why didn't you call me?" she reprimanded, then closed her lips. She knew why. "Let's take his temperature." Ellie did a quick check of the little boy, then said, "I think it's the flu, but I want a doctor to see him. You need to see one, too."

"I don't think I can make it to a doctor's office," Wyatt mumbled. "I feel really weak."

"You have to. They won't attend to Cade without you present." She found a soda cracker and gave it to Cade to chew on while she felt Wyatt's forehead. "You're burning up. What have you taken?"

"Nothing. I wanted to be here for Cade." He looked so miserable she stifled her reprimand that he wasn't much use to his son in this condition.

"We're going to the doctor," she said firmly and made a quick phone call to a doctor she knew who would see them immediately. "Gracie, you come and sit in the car with Cade. Then I'll come and help Wyatt."

"I don't need help—" He tried to rise and flopped back down in his chair.

"Of course you don't." Ellie phoned Tanner and asked him to leave the stock he was tending and come help her. She switched Cade's car seat into her car and buckled both him and Gracie in. By then Tanner was escorting Wyatt out of the house and into her car. "We'll be fine," she assured him. "But can you be here when we get back?"

"Of course." He waved them off.

Ellie drove as quickly as she could with Cade's screams filling the car.

"Sorry," Wyatt muttered before he nodded off. By the look of him it was the first sleep he'd had in a while.

At the doctor's office a passerby helped Wyatt

inside. Half an hour later they were on their way back to Wyatt's, medication in hand.

"I'm sorry." His dark eyes looked directly at her, lines of tiredness fanning out around them. "You shouldn't have had to rescue us."

"Don't be silly. Now relax. When we get home, you'll take two of those pills and go to bed," she ordered. "Gracie and I will look after Cade."

"There aren't many groceries," he muttered weakly. "And I—"

"Wyatt?"

"Yes?"

"Let me handle it." Ellie pulled into his yard and turned to look at him. "Okay?"

"Like I have a choice?" A grin flirted with his mouth before Tanner appeared to help him into the house.

"Okay, Gracie, it's time for us to get to work." Ellie carried Cade inside and, after setting some soup to warm, gave him a bath with Gracie's help. Her daughter's tender ministrations to the unhappy child touched Ellie's heart. "You'd make a great nurse, sweetheart."

"I don't want to be a nurse. I want to be a mish'nary." Gracie hummed as she showed Cade how his rubber duck could swim.

"You'll be a success at that, too," Ellie murmured. Once Cade was dressed again, she fed him a little of the soup and the medicine he'd been prescribed to settle his stomach. Then, sitting on Wyatt's porch, she rocked the little boy to sleep with Gracie nearby, playing in the sandbox as the sun slid under the horizon. "Good night, little one," she whispered, placing a kiss on his forehead.

"He's out?" Tanner stood in the doorway watching.

"For now. His fever seems to be down a bit. I think he'll rest." She carried Cade to his room and tucked him in, then returned to ask, "How's Wyatt?"

"Fussing about all the things he should be doing." Tanner frowned. "He doesn't look good."

"The doctor said he let himself get dehydrated. He needs fluids, but I didn't see much juice in the cabinets. Can you pick up some groceries?" she asked.

"Sure. Got a list?" A few minutes later he was gone.

Ellie made up a tray for Wyatt in case he was hungry. She knocked on his door, but he didn't answer. She listened closely and thought she heard him muttering, so she peeked inside. He lay sprawled on the bed in his clothes, thrashing his head from side to side.

"His fault, not just mine," he groaned. "Ted

shouldn't have been driving. He killed her. He killed Taryn. He has to pay, just like I do."

"It's okay, Wyatt," she said softly. "Everything is fine." She touched his shoulder gently, hoping to draw him out of the dream. "You're fine."

"No." He grabbed her hand and held on, his face ragged with misery, his delirium obvious. "He must be punished," he rasped.

"Leave it with God, Wyatt. It's not your burden, it's His. Forget about it now." She didn't understand exactly what was wrong but because he didn't relax she tried another approach. "Taryn's safe now. She's okay. Ted can't hurt her."

"He did, though. He should pay. God knows he should pay. I have. I've paid dearly." He kept repeating that over and over until he finally fell asleep.

Ellie tiptoed out of the room and returned to the kitchen, her mind whirling with questions. At the top of the list: How was Wyatt to blame for his wife's death?

Chapter Six

Wyatt wasn't sure what day it was or why he was still in bed when the sun was shining. All he knew was that he had to make sure Cade was all right.

But when he tried to get up, his legs wouldn't support him, and he collapsed back on his mattress.

"Everything's fine, Wyatt. Relax."

"Ellie?" He tried to clear his raspy hoarse throat, watching as she walked from the doorway toward him. "What are you doing here?"

"Looking after you and Cade. He's fine, by the way." She smiled as she set a tray on his nightstand. "Do you feel like something to eat?"

"I'm starved. And I want a cup of coffee," he said, then frowned as a thousand questions filled his head. "Why do I need looking after?"

"You don't remember getting sick?" She

waited for him to think about it, then said, "Tanner found you and Cade sick with the flu. We took you to the doctor. That was four days ago."

"Four days?" He stared at her. "I've got to get up. My stock—"

"—are fine thanks to Tanner and some folks from the church." Ellie snapped the covers around him in the crisp efficient way nurses did. "You're weak. Why don't you just relax for a bit, see if you can handle some toast and tea, then we'll talk about you getting up. Okay?"

She gave him a *strictly business* smile. Wyatt didn't like it nearly as well as the smile she always lavished on Cade.

"But I've got things to do," he protested.

"Yes, like care for your son." Ellie stared straight at him. "And you can't do that if you aren't well. Correct?"

"Fine." He reached for a piece of toast. "But I am getting up today."

"You'll have to," she shot back. "Because you're getting crumbs in that bed." The door swished closed behind her.

Wyatt chewed on the toast thoughtfully. Four days? Was that why lifting a bit of bread felt like he was hoisting a calf for branding? He managed to eat a portion, but chewing wore him out. Every single muscle in his body ached as if a bull had gored him. He leaned back against the headboard and sipped his tea. Things must be bad if he was drinking tea—and liking it.

He must have dozed off but wasn't sure how much time had passed when Ellie returned. She raised an eyebrow at the toast he'd left but lifted the tray without saying anything.

"Can I see Cade? Please?" he asked.

"Yes, of course. You must be worried about him. I'll bring him in but not for long because he's fighting his own bug. Though he is much better today." She left and returned moments later, holding Cade by the hand.

"Dada."

The sound was music to Wyatt's ears. Ellie chuckled when the little boy crowed with delight and tried to scramble onto the bed. Wyatt dearly wanted to pull his son into his arms but figured he'd embarrass himself if he tried to lift Cade.

Ellie must have noticed, because she scooped up Cade and plopped him down beside Wyatt.

"There's your daddy." The loving tenderness of her voice surprised him by its intensity. Wyatt figured he'd have to think about it later. For now, he cuddled his son next to him.

"I love you, Cade."

"You two have a little visit. I have some chores to do. Call if you need me," she said, then hurried out the door.

He was surprised by her hasty exit. Had he

done something wrong? Then Cade tugged on his shirt sleeve, and Wyatt forgot everything but the joy this little boy had brought to his life.

"How are you doing?" Ellie peeked around the door a while later. "Need a break?"

"No. He's asleep. We're good." Wyatt waited until her gaze lifted to him. "Thank you, Ellie. For everything. I don't know how I'd have managed without your help."

"God would have sent someone," she said with a shrug. "He doesn't abandon His children."

"How's Gracie?" he asked, even as he wondered if that was a safe subject.

"Mad at me." Ellie sighed, then inclined her head toward Cade. "Enjoy every moment of this stage," she advised.

"Because of the terrible twos you mean?" He saw weariness around her eyes and wished he wasn't part of the cause.

"They're nothing compared to the trying sixes. Call when you need me." She chucked Cade on the cheek, then left.

Six? Gracie must have had a birthday. But what kind of a party could she have had with her mom stuck here watching him and Cade? Wyatt figured he'd have some making up to do with the little girl once he got vertical again.

All he could do now was snuggle a sleepy

Cade by his side and do exactly as his nurse had instructed.

He could learn a lot from Ellie, Wyatt decided before sleep took over.

"When do I get to have my birthday party, Mommy?"

Same old question, same old answer.

"I don't know, honey. Soon." Ellie felt bad, but she'd been so busy taking care of Cade and Wyatt that there hadn't been time for a party. She set a plate of freshly baked cookies and a glass of milk on the counter. "Cade's having an after-school gingerbread man cookie. Want one?"

"Cade doesn't go to school." Gracie hooted with laughter. "I do." She wiggled on to the kitchen stool and, after much deliberation, picked up a cookie. "Do I have to wait till Christmas for my birthday party?" she complained in a grumpy tone. "Teacher said Christmas is only three weeks away."

"Would it be so bad to have a Christmas birthday?" Ellie asked.

"Well, me and Jesus would have a birthday on the same day," Gracie mused. Then her frown reappeared. "But I wouldn't get as many presents."

"Is that what Christmas and birthdays are about?" Ellie resisted the urge to lecture Gracie. She wanted her to figure out the meaning of Christmas on her own. "Gifts?"

"No." Gracie crunched on her cookie. "But they're very important."

"I see." Ellie continued icing the gingerbread cookies, surprised that Gracie didn't offer to help. Clearly her daughter was seriously contemplating the subject.

"Don't you like getting gifts, Mommy?" Gracie asked after she'd crunched her way through the cookie's arms and legs. "I think you do, because you laughed and smiled that time when Eddie took you for a birthday supper and gave you that big book."

"That wasn't because he gave me a gift, sweetie." Since Gracie had never spoken much about Eddie, Ellie's radar zipped to high alert. "I was happy because he did something special just for me. It meant a lot to me because I cared about him."

"And now you don't?" Those big blue eyes riveted on her, waiting for an answer.

While she considered her reply, Ellie lifted two sheets of golden cookies from the oven and set them to cool.

Making her mother's gingerbread cookies was a childhood Christmas tradition both Ellie and Karen had treasured. She would carry on the same tradition with Gracie again this year at their home, but these cookies were for Wyatt. Ellie wanted to make his Christmas more enjoyable, though she didn't want to think about why that seemed so important.

"You can tell me why you and Eddie never got married." Gracie propped her head on her palms and sighed. "I'm not a baby like Cade, Mommy."

"Yes, I know." Babies were so much easier to deal with. "Uh, Eddie is still my friend, Gracie, but in a different way. I couldn't marry him."

Gracie reached for another cookie. "Last one," she promised, correctly reading the look on her mother's puckered brow. "But *why* couldn't you marry him?"

"Because I realized I didn't love him enough." *Not enough to put you in a boarding school.* As if traveling the world could compare with raising Gracie. "I told you all this," she reminded her daughter.

"No, Mommy." Grace shook her head, her icing-covered face solemn. "You only said we weren't gonna be a fam'ly." She finished her milk. "I wanted to ask why, but you were so sad so I didn't." She climbed off the stool. "But now you're happier," she said before she headed for the bathroom to wash up.

Ellie tried to puzzle out what Gracie meant.

"Is she right? Are you happier now?" Wyatt leaned against the doorjamb, his face pale.

"Come and sit down before you fall down." Ellie was prepared to rush over to lend a shoulder, but Wyatt made it on his own. His hair was damp. "You took a shower?"

"I needed one. Don't fuss." He picked up a cookie and took a bite.

"A nurse does not *fuss*," she said in a stern tone. "And a cookie is hardly the first thing you should be putting in your empty stomach."

"I'd put coffee in there if you made some. Please?" He grinned at her. "And you're dodging my question."

"Which was?" She avoided his scrutiny by turning to the coffeemaker.

"Are you happier now?" Wyatt wiped off his son's face and hands and lifted him down from his high chair. "Now that you're not with this Eddie person anymore?"

"Wyatt, that's kind of personal." Ellie tried to regain her composure while she poured a cup of coffee and set it in front of him.

"You've seen me at my worst. Cared for my sick kid. What's a little more personal stuff between friends?"

"Uh—" Ellie looked around for a way to escape.

"I think Mommy would be more happier if she put me in the wooden school." Gracie came in and flopped on to the floor to play blocks with Cade.

Aghast, Ellie stared at her daughter. She'd been so careful, trying to ensure Gracie would never know she'd been the reason for the breakup with Eddie. Well, part of the reason.

"Wooden school?" Wyatt's gaze shifted from Gracie to Ellie. "What's that?"

"It's school for kids who can't live at home 'cause their moms aren't there." Gracie sounded nonchalant. "I asked my Sunday school teacher."

"Boarding school," Ellie explained for Wyatt's benefit. "I wish you'd told me you overheard that, Gracie."

"I couldn't tell you. You'd have cried more. I don't like it when you cry, Mommy." She looked at Ellie, her face utterly serious. "But I *could* go there. Then you and Eddie could get married."

"Gracie, honey, Eddie and I don't want to get married."

"He might want to if I went to the wooden school." It was obvious she'd thought about this a lot. "If I went there you could ask him. You'd hafta say please," she warned. Then her bottom lip began to tremble. "'Cept I'd really miss Melissa. An' Wranglers Ranch." She gulped. "An' you," she whispered as a big shiny tear dribbled down her cheek.

"Oh, darling." Ellie swallowed the lump in her

throat as she rushed across the room and knelt to hug her precious little girl close to her heart. She didn't have to worry. Gracie knew all about giving gifts. And she'd just given her mom a priceless one. "It's very kind of you to offer, but I don't want to marry Eddie."

"Sure?" Gracie sniffed.

"Positive." Ellie swiped away her tears, her heart brimming with love. "I keep telling you, darling. You and I are a family. We always will be, even when you grow up and get married and have your own children."

Gracie's smile blazed with relief, but a moment later her eyes turned troubled. "I can't get married," she wailed. "I don't got no daddy."

"What does having a father have to do with getting married?" Wyatt asked.

"Miss Carter, she's my teacher," Gracie explained with a sniff. "She said her daddy is going to walk her into the church when she gets married. She said all daddies do that. But I don't got a daddy to walk me, so I can't never get married." Fresh tears poured from her eyes.

Ellie leaned back on her heels and glared at Wyatt, whose peals of laughter filled the room.

"Gracie, honey, you have a very long time before you have to think about marriage. Let's not worry about that now."

Gracie sniffed as she considered this. "'Kay,"

she finally agreed. She brushed away her tears and began gathering blocks. "Cade, you an' me are gonna build a church where people get married. Only not Mommy and Eddie."

Sighing, Ellie rose and rescued the last of her cookies from the oven.

"Escaped that by the skin of your teeth, Ellie Grant." Wyatt's eyes crinkled with his smile. "But don't think I don't expect an answer. About your happiness," he whispered with a check over one shoulder to be sure Gracie didn't overhear. "Or lack thereof."

"Did you know there are certain kinds of poison you can add to food which are totally undetectable?" Ellie methodically stirred the pot of soup on the stove. "The person who eats it never even knows it's their last meal." She glanced at Wyatt over one shoulder. "Totally oblivious."

She hid her smile at his gaping stare and calmly set out four bowls and four spoons to go along with her freshly baked bread.

"Supper's in an hour," she said brightly. "If you're strong enough to watch the kids for a bit, I think I'll go for a walk."

When Wyatt finally managed a nod, Ellie left, inhaling deeply as she strode down the drive.

Wasn't it funny that the thought of marrying Eddie no longer held any attraction? He was part of the past, a part she could forget and not mourn.

What wasn't funny was that she'd begun to have silly dreams about living here, on Wyatt's ranch, watching the spectacular sunsets with him, seeing him raise his son, listening to that full-bodied laugh.

"God, I'm really trying to manage Gracie on my own, to keep us strong as a family and find contentment in the life You want for me," she whispered as she strolled among the lacy mesquite trees. "But I think I'm getting too fond of Cade." *And Wyatt.* "It sure would be nice if You could heal Wyatt so Gracie and I can get back to our own lives."

Ellie really meant that. But she had a hunch that from now on, being a single mom wasn't going to be quite as fulfilling as it once had been.

"You have to be on your best behavior tonight," Wyatt told his son two evenings later. "No spilling, no yelling. There will be ladies present. Okay?"

Cade gave him a baleful look. "Dada. Meem." Meem was Cade's word for more.

"No more juice right now," Wyatt told him. "We have to get going." He sniffed, then made a detour to change his son. "One of these days, when you're a little older, you and I are going to have a heart-to-heart about how to attract girls. This isn't it."

Cade blew a raspberry.

"That won't impress them either. And you'll only be able to get by on those baby-face good looks for so long, kid. Trust me, it's not easy when you get older."

Wyatt paused. Was that what he was doing, trying to impress Ellie? A surge of guilt rose as he glanced at his wedding picture and Taryn. No, he wasn't looking to get involved again. No way. It was just that Ellie—

He shoved the thought away, did one more check to be sure he had everything, then he headed out the door. He was just pulling up at Ellie's place when his phone rang.

"Hey, Wyatt. Where are you?"

"Hey, Tanner. At Ellie's. We should be there in ten minutes. Everything ready?"

"And waiting," came Tanner's response. Then he hung up.

Ellie and her daughter were waiting outside, so Wyatt jumped out to help Gracie into the backseat beside Cade. When she was buckled in he moved to the passenger side and held Ellie's door, closing it once she was inside.

"What's going on, Wyatt?" she asked after fastening her seat belt. "Where are we going?"

"You'll see." She tried to probe further, but he avoided her questions. "Here we are," he said a few minutes later as they drove through the gates to Wranglers Ranch.

"Mommy, my name is on that sign. What does the rest say?" Gracie asked, pointing to a banner attached to the fence and lit up by the yard light.

"It says *Happy Birthday, Gracie*," Wyatt told her. "I hope you don't mind, but since you couldn't have a birthday party because Cade and I were sick and keeping your mom busy, I made you one. This is your birthday party." He pulled in and parked, laughing out loud at her squeal of surprise when a clown appeared and opened her door. "Happy birthday, Gracie."

The clown lifted Gracie down from the truck, then he produced a crown and set it on her head. He bowed in front of her, then blew on a whistle. Suddenly lights, thousands of them, blinked to life on a huge Christmas tree. The clown took Gracie's hand, and as he led her toward the tree, candy canes glowed to life, lighting up a path.

"Shall we?" Wyatt asked Ellie. He was a bit worried by her silence. But when he opened the door, and the interior lights clicked on, he saw she was crying. "I blew it, didn't I?" he said, utterly devastated by those tears.

"Are you kidding me? You are the most amazing man..." Ellie dashed away her tears, leaned over and kissed him hard and fast. Then she jerked away, flushed a bright Christmas red and clapped a hand over her mouth. A second later she recovered enough to say, "This is the nicest thing you could have done for her. Thank you, Wyatt."

"You're welcome." He grinned and quashed the desire to return her kiss. Friends, that's all they were. "Shall we join the party?" At her nod he unbuckled Cade, and they joined Gracie.

"Come on," she called with a frantic wave. "Mr. Clown says we hafta follow the candy canes."

As they walked through what he hoped looked like an enchanted forest where even the cacti had been dressed for the event, Wyatt couldn't help watching Ellie's reaction. She was as much a kid as Gracie, her head twisting from one side to the other to take it all in. She stopped short at one point and gazed upward.

"Snowflakes," she whispered. "How perfect."

"Perfect?" He was puzzled by the comment. "In Tucson?"

"Perfect for me." Ellie tilted her head, as if she was waiting for one of the white plastic snowflakes to fall so she could catch it on her tongue. "I was born and raised in North Dakota. We always had snow at Christmas. It's the one thing

I still miss." She looked at him. "And you managed to re-create it in the desert."

"With some help." He steered Cade back on to the path. "It's the least I could do for making Gracie miss her birthday."

"And you said you couldn't decorate." Ellie made a face at him. "How long did it take you to make all these snowflakes?"

"I can't decorate, and I didn't make them. Taryn kept the snowflakes from some hospital fund-raising gig she did once. They were sitting in boxes in the garage so… Tanner helped me put them up."

"They're beautiful. Oh, look!" Ellie grabbed his hand, her face every bit as excited as Gracie's when she spied the blow-up snowman. "It's so cute." She stopped short when a group of kids began to sing "Happy Birthday" to Gracie.

Wyatt stood beside Ellie, enjoying the myriad expressions that flickered across her face. "I hope it's okay that I invited her whole class. I didn't want to leave out anyone. Her teacher helped."

"You invited twenty-two kids to Wranglers Ranch and Tanner let you?" she said.

"Actually he suggested it. He also hired the bus to bring them here. Apparently the parents will pick them up at eight o'clock." Wyatt smothered a surge of pleasure at Ellie's surprise and obvious enjoyment as she mingled among the kids.

"It's amazing," she breathed when she returned from circulating. "A bouncy castle. A clown and those little ponies—where did they come from?"

"I mentioned to Tanner that one of my clients is selling his place. His buyer doesn't want the miniatures, so now they have a new home on Wranglers Ranch." Wyatt smiled as Gracie climbed on one with Lefty's help. "Tanner thinks they'll be perfect for the smaller kids to ride. I checked them over. They're all healthy."

Ellie watched as the kids went squealing from one activity to the next. When she finally turned to face him, there was a look on her face that Wyatt couldn't decipher.

"Tanner was right," she murmured.

"About?" he prodded.

"You working for Wranglers Ranch. Look how this place has blossomed since you started. Tanner told me you caught two infections another vet missed." She studied him, her face serious. "Your suggestions are amazing. You should come on board full-time."

"Tanner's asked me, but I have my practice to run." Cade dragged at his hand, wanting to go to the horses. So, with one of Wranglers' hands holding the reins, Wyatt lifted his son on to the smallest horse and walked beside it. "Look at him," he crowed with pride. "A true cowboy through and through."

"I suppose you'll be entering Cade in the rodeo in February," Ellie teased a few minutes later. "Seriously though Wyatt, why don't you think about working here?"

"I'm committed to building my own business." She didn't have to know he'd lost another client this week.

"A laudable goal for sure," she said quietly.

"But?" Since Cade was drooping Wyatt lifted him off the horse and carried him to the drinks table. "You don't think I can do it?"

"Of course you can do it," Ellie said firmly. "It's more a question of do you want to? Full-time work here would give you more regular hours. You could spend evenings and weekends with this guy, mostly uninterrupted." She tickled Cade and laughed when he giggled. "He won't nap in the afternoon forever."

"I know but—" Wyatt wanted her to understand, but he wasn't sure he wanted to explain why he needed to build his business. "I must have my own business, Ellie."

"Okay. So why can't part of your business be as the on-call vet for Wranglers? I know Tanner has asked you several times." Her eyes held his, waiting for his response. "Don't you like working here?"

"I love it." He was embarrassed by how fast that response slipped out. "It's a fantastic place to work. Tanner knows his stuff, and he treats his animals well. He takes my suggestions seriously, and I'm very proud to be associated with his work with the kids that come here." He grinned. "Plus, he's a great spiritual mentor, and I need that."

"So what's the problem?"

"I guess I could agree to be his on-call vet." He shrugged. "That's basically what I'm doing now anyway, and so far it's working well. I don't mind the extra income either."

"That's good to hear. I'm sure he'll be pleased." It looked like she was, too. "We'll enjoy whatever time you can spend here. You'll be a great asset to Wranglers."

Wyatt was about to thank her when he noticed her attention had turned to Gracie. As Ellie moved closer he followed, noting her frown as they both overheard Gracie tell another child how she'd prayed for a special birthday party.

"And God answered." She glanced around with a happy grin. "Isn't it great? He'll answer my other prayers, too," she added, her attention now focused on Wyatt. "I know it."

Seeing that Ellie was about to have words with

her daughter, Wyatt stepped in. "Gracie, are you ready for your cake?" He hoped the fairy-tale cake Sophie was setting on the table would divert her attention.

Wyatt moved behind Ellie, breathing in her fragrance as a light breeze tossed stands of her hair across his face. Standing there contentedly as he watched Gracie blow out the candles, he couldn't help but marvel at the little girl's faith. She had implicit trust in God to answer her prayers. Ellie seemed the same. Both of them expected God to be there for them.

Wyatt wanted to share that trust. Longed to.

But how can God give you your dreams when you still blame that boy for Taryn's death? When you can't trust Him with that?

They were sobering questions. Ones he didn't have the answers to. Yet.

Chapter Seven

"Mommy?"

"Yes, honey?" Relieved that Gracie's star was finally perched atop their Christmas tree, Ellie carefully lifted her daughter down.

Getting the star in place on Monday morning before work and school wasn't exactly the way she'd planned to finish the weekend job of decorating their tree but at least it was one less thing on her list. With only two and a half weeks left before Christmas, that list seemed endless.

"Can we go to… Cade's house after school today?"

Ellie gathered her daughter's backpack and ushered her out to the car. "Wyatt told me at your party that he has a sitter for Cade in the afternoons now. We don't need to go there anymore."

Ellie knew she should be grateful for that freedom because every second of her day was filled with things to do. Only she missed those visits. A lot. And not just because of Cade.

"But I *need* to go to Cade's house to see him and his daddy," she insisted.

"Why?" Might as well get it out in the open, Ellie decided in resignation.

"To find out what to get them for Christmas." Gracie said it as if Ellie should have known. "We haven't got them a gift yet."

"I wasn't thinking we would." Ellie didn't have the resources to *buy* that many gifts. "Anyway, Cade couldn't tell you, and I'm sure Wyatt won't either."

"I'm not going to *ask* them." Gracie looked at her askance. "I'm just going to see what they need."

"Oh." Ellie coughed to cover her mirth.

"'Sides, Da—" Gracie peeked at her, then quickly adjusted to say, "—*he's* going to let me help him with a hurt owl."

"Wyatt. His name is Wyatt. Or Mr. Wright." Exasperated, Ellie pulled into the school lot. "When did he say that?"

"At church. Yesterday." Gracie grinned. "I liked helping him with the animals."

As if she'd done it more than twice.

"We can't go today," Ellie insisted. "I have too much to do before Christmas."

"When then?" Gracie stared at her, waiting for an answer Ellie didn't have.

"I don't know. We'll see. Now off you go so you aren't late." She pulled into the drop-off zone, leaned back and kissed her cheek. "Bye, sweetie."

"Can I go tomorrow?" Gracie asked as she exited the car.

"We'll talk about it later." *When the answer would still be no.*

Gracie's over-the-top-birthday party on Friday night, a camp at Wranglers Ranch on Saturday, which he'd helped with, and yesterday when he'd sat beside her in church—Ellie had been seeing entirely too much of Wyatt Wright lately.

Not that she wasn't grateful to him. She was. That party had been an incredibly kind and generous gesture to a little girl.

But lately it seemed Wyatt was at Wranglers Ranch every day, which meant she talked to him every day and admired him working with the animals *every day*. She'd lectured herself a hundred times about it and still couldn't shake this silly schoolgirl crush on him. It seemed like her no-romance rule was in danger of being breached, and that wasn't going to happen. She wouldn't, couldn't let it.

By the time she arrived at the ranch she was

ten minutes late, and Tanner was waiting in her tiny log house/office.

"I'm sorry I'm late," she apologized.

Ignoring her apology, he blurted, "Sophie's sick." The miserable look on his face said it all. "Nothing I do helps."

"Morning sickness," she guessed. "I'll go make her some peppermint tea."

"Thank you, Ellie." Tanner's sunny smile reappeared. "I knew you'd know what to do. And if Wyatt comes looking for me, tell him I'm in the north quarter trying to figure out how that coyote got in."

"Any damage?" There must have been if Wyatt had been called.

"It bit one of the pregnant mares, which means a tetanus shot and probably some antibiotics." He made a face. "Lefty's tracking the coyote in case it's sick."

"Okay, I'll tell Wyatt." Ellie walked to the main house trying not to skip as she went. What in the world was wrong with her that thoughts of Wyatt made her act like Gracie?

After reading herself the riot act, she took Sophie the tea she'd brewed, her heart saddened by the mom-to-be's stricken look as she lay in bed, her face whiter than her sheets.

"Drink this," Ellie said handing her the cup. "And munch on those crackers."

"I'm a nuisance," Sophie groaned. "And I'm so tired."

"It will pass. Drink the tea." Ellie waited until she'd taken a sip. "You don't have any catering jobs today, do you?"

"Nothing till the weekend. Thank You, Lord." Sophie lay back on the pillows. "I'd forgotten all about morning sickness."

"And you will again when this baby's born," Ellie promised. "Rest now."

In the kitchen she cleaned up the counters, turned on the dishwasher and started a slow-cooker meal for Sophie and Tanner's lunch. She was about to leave when she saw Wyatt drive up.

Settle down, she told her dancing stomach. *It's only Wyatt.*

Only Wyatt. Right. Mocking herself, Ellie stepped outside and closed the door behind her. She set a little Do Not Disturb sign on the step.

"Good morning." He glanced from the sign to her, a question in his eyes.

"Morning sickness. She'll sleep for a while." Ellie couldn't help studying Wyatt with an approving glance. He looked fresh and ready to take on the day, his usually bristled jaw clean, revealing his sharp chin and full lips. He must iron his shirts to get them so crisp. And where in Tucson did they sell jeans that fit like that?

"Ellie?"

"Sorry." She tried to hide her blush. "Uh, Tanner said you could find him in the north quarter."

"Hunting for the coyote, I expect." He frowned when she kept standing there. "Is anything wrong?"

"No." She scanned her fuzzy brain for something to explain her fog. "Just that, well, I was wondering..." This was going to sound so awkward, especially since yesterday she'd refused his lunch offer because she'd been trying to distance herself. "Is there a good time when I could bring Gracie over to your place?"

Surprise widened his eyes.

"She wants to help you with an owl." Relieved when understanding dawned, she added, "And find out what to get you and Cade for Christmas."

"Oh, that's not necessary."

"I'm afraid it is to her," Ellie told him. "Can we walk and talk?" He nodded, so she led the way to her office. "Gracie has this thing about Christmas gifts."

"Thing?" Wyatt arched an eyebrow.

"She's been making a list of gifts she wants to give," she explained. "In fact now she wants to give one to each of the friends she's made here at the ranch."

"But surely you can't afford that." Wyatt blinked. "What I mean is—"

"I know what you mean, and you're right that I can't buy that many gifts." She smiled. "Fortunately we're making decorated gingerbread people. A little bag of cookies for each friend."

"That's a lot of work." He stopped outside the door.

"Especially since my place is so small. The kitchen is dinky and the oven even smaller. I was going to ask Sophie to use the kitchen here until I found out how much Christmas catering she has booked. I don't want to add to her stress."

"You tell Gracie those cookies would make a great gift for Cade and me, too." Wyatt grinned.

"Uh, I don't think cookies will cut it with Gracie, though you could try suggesting it."

"But I don't want her to spend her money on us."

"Wyatt, you should know by now that there's no point in telling me to stop Gracie," Ellie said with asperity. "It's like telling a horse not to eat grass."

Wyatt's laughter reached to the top of the Palo Verde tree outside her door. "Don't I know it." He sobered. "What does Gracie want for Christmas?"

"I think you already know that answer," she said, keeping her face expressionless.

"She's still harping on about a daddy for

Christmas?" Her nod made Wyatt groan. "I was hoping we'd moved past that by now."

"You wish." Ellie needed to prepare for a new class of troubled kids who'd been court-mandated to spend time at Wranglers. Tanner's successful equine assisted rehabilitation program was getting high marks from those who worked with kids at risk. Still, she stood there studying the handsome veterinarian.

"You have quite a daughter." Wyatt's gaze held hers for so long Ellie wondered if she was the only one that felt the air simmering between them. Eventually he said, "I better stop gabbing and go find Tanner. See you, Ellie." He waved, then walked away.

Ellie forced herself to enter her office knowing he'd saddle up and ride cross-country to find Tanner, which was quicker and easier than driving the rugged foothills. It took every bit of self-control she had, but she refused to go to the window and watch him ride off.

She couldn't help it if her brain noted the sound of his horse trotting away, or that she couldn't focus until she heard the same trot signalling his return. She was going to have to do something about this ridiculous fixation on Wyatt Wright.

Before it got out of control.

* * *

Wyatt ended his call and shoved his phone into his pocket while trying to stifle the guilt that always rose whenever he left Cade with a sitter. But Tanner had offered him an afternoon's work, and he couldn't turn it down. Besides, according to the sitter, Cade was having a ball in the sandbox.

"Kids who've had encounters with the justice system are sometimes desperate to vent, and they take it out on the animals. I'd appreciate it if you could stay today, Wyatt, just in case something crops up," Tanner had said earlier, so Wyatt had agreed to stay until the class was finished.

Now he stood beside Ellie outside the tack room, watching as a bunch of trying-to-be-tough teens fumbled and bumbled with the equipment they'd been given to groom their horses.

"Who exactly are these kids?" he asked sotto voce.

"Kids who've had some kind of brush with the law. Not hardened criminals, which is why they're here," she explained. "Tanner's program has had a lot of success breaking down the barriers that troubled kids usually have."

Wyatt immediately thought of the kid he knew only as Ted, the boy he blamed for Taryn's death, and felt a surge of anger. He sure hoped no judge sent that kid here to play with horses as punishment.

"Have you given any more thought to Tanner's offer of full-time employment?" Ellie asked.

"You mean because I'm around Wranglers so much?" He chuckled at her sheepish face. "It's very attractive but—"

"You still feel you have to build your own business." She frowned. "You *are* here a lot."

Brutal, but it was the truth. "I can't accept Tanner's offer."

"Why? Can you tell me?" Ellie's kind eyes studied him. It was the compassion Wyatt saw there that drew his response.

"I made a promise to my dad before he died that I would make mine the best veterinarian business in Tucson, worthy of the Wright name." He saw her lips purse. "What?"

"It's none of my business, of course, but I don't think it's fair for parents to put those kinds of restrictions on their kids. What parent can know the future choices their kid will have to make?" Ellie sounded annoyed.

"What did your parents do?" he asked curiously.

"They told us that it didn't matter to them what career we chose. They said they'd be proud of us as long as we were the best that we could be." Ellie nodded. "I think that's what every parent should want for their child."

Wyatt thought about that for a moment, about how sensible it sounded. "You had a good childhood, didn't you, Ellie?"

"The best." Her face transformed into pure happiness. "We never had much money. Dad farmed. Mom helped him and took in sewing for people. But they always had time for us, and we had so much fun together." Her face sobered. "My parents gave my sister and me things money can't buy, like boundless love, joy and encouragement. They're both gone now, but we never doubted we were loved. That's what I want for Gracie." She sighed. "And that's what I can't seem to instill in her."

"Why do you say that?" Wyatt hated that sound of defeat. "Gracie knows you love her."

"But it's not enough. She's still trying to find security by finding a daddy," Ellie said, her pain obvious. "I'm doing something wrong."

Wyatt didn't have time to dispute that because Tanner waved him over to help with one of the kids, a barely-teenage boy named Albert. Seeing the kid's embarrassment and shyness, Wyatt joked as he demonstrated how to untangle the reins so the horse could move its head more freely. As he did he tried to ease Albert's obvious nervousness. But all the while Wyatt couldn't forget Ellie's face when she'd spoken of her parents, because that was exactly how he wanted Cade to feel about him.

By the time the class left, Wyatt was glad to share the coffee and snacks Sophie offered. Clearly much recovered, she was baking Christmas goodies. Tanner stayed to talk to her while Wyatt and Ellie went to the patio for their coffee break.

"That boy you were working with. Albert? Did you notice the marks on his arms?" Ellie sat, her troubled tone drawing Wyatt's attention. "When he bent to treat his horse's hooves, his shirt bagged, and I saw bruises all over his chest. And he winced when one of the other kids slung their arm over his shoulder."

Tears filled her eyes and rolled down her cheeks. Her pain clenched his insides.

"Ellie!" he exclaimed. "What's wrong?"

"Those marks—I've seen them before. Lots of times in the pediatric wards." She bit her bottom lip. "Albert avoided answering my questions about how he got those marks. He said he's fine, his home life is fine. Everything is fine."

"You don't believe him?"

She shook her head. "I think Albert is being abused." She looked as though the words had been pulled from her lips, her face heart-wrenchingly sad.

"Did you tell Tanner?"

She sniffed, then nodded.

"And?"

"He said I should call his social worker and ask her to investigate. So I did." Ellie burst into fresh tears. "It's horrible to think about, isn't it? That sweet, gentle kid being used as someone's punching bag. I hated these cases when I worked pediatrics."

Unable to bear seeing this caring woman so broken up, Wyatt moved to sit beside her and drew her into his arms.

"It's okay," he soothed. "You did the right thing. Now things will get better for him. They'll investigate, find the truth and move Albert somewhere safe," he said, trying to comfort her. But Ellie slowly shook her head from side to side. "It won't get better for him?"

"It doesn't always. Adults in these situations can be devious." She drew away. Funny how empty his arms felt without her in them. "You don't believe me, but I've heard it before. Trust me, the story will be something like this, 'Albert needed discipline and struggled when we tried to get him to obey, so we had to restrain him.' It's always a variation like that."

"And you're worried?" he guessed.

"Wyatt, I saw the marks at the back of his neck. I'm positive they were bruises from thumb prints." Her voice lowered. "There is no good explanation for that. What if they hurt him more seriously?"

"The social worker's been warned," he said as he tried to put it all together. "She'll be on the lookout now."

"I may have made it worse by reporting it." Her face whitened even more.

"Ellie, you had to. Given your suspicions you couldn't have done nothing. Could you?" He brushed her silky curls off her face to peer into her eyes. Slowly she shook her head.

"No. I had to tell."

"So now there's nothing more you can do." Some tiny glimmer in her eyes made Wyatt add, "Is there?"

"I don't know." She didn't look at him, stared instead at her hands clenched in her lap. "Maybe."

"What do you mean?" Wyatt had a hunch he wasn't going to like this.

"Albert's group is scheduled to return twice more this week, Wednesday and Friday." Ellie's shoulders went back. "I'm going to keep a close eye on him, and if I see further signs of abuse, I—"

"What?" Dread tiptoed up his back. "What are you thinking?"

"I might visit him at home." She stared directly into his eyes, her resolve firm.

"Ellie," he warned, his admiration for her rivaling his concern. "You can't just waltz—"

"Mommy doesn't know how to waltz, do you, Mommy?" Gracie stood behind them. When they twisted to face her, she frowned. "Did you make my mommy cry?" she demanded of Wyatt, her gaze frosty.

"No!" Wyatt didn't get a chance to explain.

"Of course he didn't. And you know it's rude to eavesdrop, Gracie." Ellie rose, straightened her shirt and brushed a hand across her cheeks. "I was just sad about something, and Wyatt was—er, helping me feel better."

"You know, that's exactly what I was going to tell her." Sophie stood in the doorway of the house, a big grin spread across her face. She winked at Wyatt, then said, "Gracie, honey, I saw you get off the bus. Beth will be here soon. Do you want to come and taste one of my star cookies while you wait?"

"Sure." Gracie dropped her backpack and loped toward Sophie.

"I'd better get back to work. I need to clean my office," Ellie said, speaking quickly as if she was embarrassed by Sophie's teasing.

"Yeah, that kid who cut his hand on the curry brush made a mess waving all over the place."

Wyatt grinned. "I never knew anyone could cut their hand on a curry brush."

"He did seem a little accident-prone, didn't he?"

"Maybe that's what happened to this Albert kid?" he suggested.

"I have no doubt that someone will suggest that," she said quietly.

"Promise me something, Ellie." If you couldn't beat the Grant women, you could only join them. Wyatt exhaled. "If you do decide to go to this Albert's place, will you let me know, so I can go with you?"

"You? Why?" She looked stunned.

"Because I don't want you to walk into a situation where you could get hurt," he said gruffly.

"You think his relatives would try to hurt me?" Clearly that hadn't occurred to her.

"That's the thing. You don't know. Neither do I. If it's as bad as you think, anything could happen." He held her gaze. "So you'll tell me, right? And we'll go together."

She studied him for a long time before she finally nodded. A smile lifted her lips. "Thank you, Wyatt."

"You're welcome. Now I've got to get home." He turned and almost tripped over Gracie who was crunching on a cookie with vivid red icing spread across her face.

"Can I go with you?" she asked, her mouth full.

"What? Why?" Gracie's sudden reappearance left Wyatt feeling slightly off-kilter.

"To help with the owl, remember?" She licked her lips and rubbed her messy hands on her jeans. "And I want to see that old billy goat with the bad leg. An'..."

She trailed away on a nonstop sentence that included almost every animal on his ranch.

"I can't go there today, Gracie," Ellie said. "Tanner wants to talk to me."

"I want to talk to Wyatt, too." Tanner stepped up to them and smiled at Gracie. "Beth's bus is here. Can you play with her while I talk to your mom?"

"'Kay." She pinned Wyatt with a warning look. "I want to see the owl," she said firmly, then left.

"You know, Tanner, you and Gracie need to stop creeping up on people," Wyatt complained when she'd left. "It makes me nervous."

"Must be your guilty conscience." Tanner sniggered at the menacing look Wyatt shot him. "I had a phone call today from your favorite organization, Ellie."

"Make-A-Wish Arizona? So they did call." She grinned, then explained to Wyatt. "They're a group I volunteer with. They've been trying to arrange Christmas wishes for some of their terminally sick kids."

"Ellie suggested Wranglers Ranch could help with that." Tanner scratched his chin. "They want to bring four children the day before Christmas Eve."

"Why do you need me?" Wyatt asked.

"Because these specific children probably can't ride our horses as other kids do. Of course, there'll be attendants for them, all that kind of thing," Tanner explained. "But apparently they'll need modifications and adaptations, and I'd like your input. They also want assurances that someone will be on hand to guarantee the horses are safe and that Ellie's here to deal with any potential incident."

"Understandably, they are very big on safety." Ellie said.

Tanner nodded. "I really want to do this. If Wranglers Ranch can bring some Christmas joy to children who are fighting for their lives, then we ought to do it."

"So...?" Wyatt glanced from him to Ellie, noting that the shadows were gone, and her gray eyes now sparkled with anticipation.

"Wyatt, I want to hire you for the next two and a half weeks to work with five specific animals that the children may ride," Tanner said. "I don't want even a risk of a problem with my animals, because if this works out, I'd like to do it more often."

"We can get their doctors' suggestions as to what's needed, because some kids will need adaptations of the saddles." Ellie's earnest voice begged Wyatt to agree. "We'll have to make sure everything complies if we're going to make this Christmas special for them."

"I also want some contacts from you, Wyatt." Tanner pulled out a notepad and pen. "I loved the way Wranglers Ranch added to Gracie's birthday party. I'd like to try and re-create it for two other 'Wish' kids who may visit." He paused, then lifted an eyebrow. "So, what do you say? Can you give us the time?"

Should he? Wyatt knew he needed to distance himself from the lovely Ellie, not spend more time with her. But he couldn't say no to suffering kids. What were a couple of weeks of his time? If it were Cade…

"I'm in," he promised.

"Good. We'll start preparations tomorrow." Tanner tapped his pen. "Now, what's the phone number of that clown you hired for Gracie's party? He was great."

Wyatt answered, but his attention wasn't on Tanner, it was on Ellie. She worked with young kids in Sunday school. She worked with troubled kids and school groups, and now she'd be there for sick kids who came here to Wranglers Ranch. She was determined to go out of her way for this kid named Albert whom she'd only met once. She'd cared for Cade, and she also had a daughter who needed her. Ellie gave and she gave and she gave.

For all of those reasons, and a hundred more that he wasn't going to enumerate right now, Wyatt really liked this woman. And he was determined to keep his promise to be here to help with the Make-A-Wish kids.

But then you'll have to back away, because you don't keep your promises. You haven't even kept the one you made your dad ten years ago. Do not let this woman or her precocious daughter get under your skin, because you will disappoint her, just as you disappointed Taryn.

Later, as Wyatt drove home with Gracie singing to Cade about owls, he caught himself anticipating dinner with Ellie, and he wondered if that mental warning hadn't come just a bit too late.

Chapter Eight

"I feel sorry for him." Two evenings later Ellie felt like she'd lost her Christmas spirit.

Wyatt sat at his kitchen table beside Gracie who was cutting out Christmas cookies for her gifts. It had been so decent of him to offer her his kitchen with its double ovens to work in. Ellie knew she should be happy that Gracie's cookie list was getting finished and yet…

"You feel sorry for who?"

"Albert. He didn't look much better today, did he?" Ellie plopped three silver candy beads down the front of a gingerbread boy. "I wonder if it's my fault."

"Did you do something bad, Mommy?" Gracie frowned at the star she'd mashed.

"I'm not sure yet." Ellie wished she hadn't mentioned it with little ears listening. "Can I help you, honey?" When her daughter nodded,

Ellie took the cutter from her hand, reformed the last bits of dough and quickly pressed out the star.

"It will look pretty with this blue sugar on it," Gracie said.

"Very nice," Ellie approved. "Now we're finished for tonight, so you go wash up. Quietly because, remember, Cade's sleeping. As soon as these are baked, we need to get you home to bed, too."

Gracie did an exaggerated tiptoe to the bathroom, making Wyatt smile.

"She didn't argue. She must be tired." Ellie moved quickly to clean up and then started the dishwasher. "Thank you so much for letting Gracie help you with the animals and for allowing me to use your house as my workshop," she said over one shoulder as she removed two more cookie sheets from the oven. "This baking is going a lot faster than I ever imagined."

"How many more batches do you need?" Wyatt asked, snitching one of the cookies for a taste test.

"Maybe three more." She grinned at his surprised face. "Gracie's list is huge."

"But—"

"I know it's overkill," Ellie defended. "But I want to encourage her giving spirit. I like that she's thought about these kids, thought about how many of them might not receive much for Christmas, especially something homemade. She's trying, in her way, to make it special for them. I don't want to crush that."

"And Albert?" Wyatt arched one eyebrow when she didn't immediately respond.

"I'm wondering if my speaking up made his life worse." She took a sip of the coffee she'd made earlier. "I'm going to visit his home."

"Ellie, I don't think—" Wyatt stopped speaking when Gracie returned. A muscle in his jaw flickered, but all he said was, "When?"

"Maybe on the weekend." She slid the cooled cookies into a big tin she'd brought and snapped on the lid. "Sweetheart, do you think you can put this tin inside the cooler I left on the doorstep?"

"Sure." Holding the tin as if it was pure gold, Gracie walked out of the room.

"I'm not keen on kids who've been in trouble with the law spending time at Wranglers," Wyatt muttered. "Seems like they get off too easily."

"Tanner's programs are for troubled kids, not necessarily those mandated to attend by the courts." Ellie frowned. "You're thinking of the boy who was involved in Taryn's accident, aren't you?" She could see from his expression that she'd guessed right. "What do you know about him?"

"Not much." His tone was sour. "I never heard

any details in the press, but then again, he was a juvenile."

"You were burying Taryn and busy with Cade. I doubt you had much time to watch the news for details," she soothed.

"At the time I didn't think much about it." He crunched hard on the rest of his cookie. "A police officer said there was a group of kids who'd been driving illegally and mentioned the driver's name once. Ted. That's all I know about him."

"Ah, that's who Ted is," she murmured.

"You know him?" Wyatt asked in surprise.

"No." Ellie wondered if she should have said anything. But Wyatt's stare had to be answered. "You spoke of him when you were sick. I think you must have been dreaming."

"About the night Taryn died." He stared at his hands. "It happens sometimes." Then his voice dropped. "Probably because I can't get rid of my guilt. Or the anger toward this Ted for what he did."

"If you're still dreaming about him, the anger is eating at you." She sensed the anger had festered since the accident. "I'm sorry for you, Wyatt. But I also feel sorry for him. It must be horrible to carry such a burden. Can't you free yourself by forgiving him?"

"No," he refused in a hard tone.

"It's not my business, and maybe you think I

should be quiet, but I have to say this. Christians are commanded to forgive. I think it's mostly so we don't harbor ill will that eats at us." She studied him with a troubled look. "Besides, God has forgiven us for so much. How can we not forgive others? Sooner or later you have to let it go, Wyatt."

"He has to pay," Wyatt insisted in an irritated voice. "We all do."

"Maybe. But when will Ted, or you," she added, "have paid enough?"

Wyatt got suddenly quiet, so she forced a smile at Gracie who had returned. "Gather up your coloring things and put them in your backpack. These are the last pans. We just have to wait for them to cool a bit, then we'll head home."

Ellie noticed Gracie covertly studying Wyatt as she packed her things. After a time her daughter asked, "What are you getting Cade for Christmas?"

"Gracie, that's—"

"I don't know." Wyatt looked at her warily. "Why?"

"'Cause I know the perfect thing." Gracie grinned. "Cade would love a puppy."

"I see. Why do you think that, Gracie?" Wyatt lifted her onto his knee. "Is that what you want for Christmas?"

His tender voice brought a lump to Ellie's

throat, which grew when Gracie cupped a hand on his cheek and shook her head.

"You don't like puppies?" Wyatt asked.

"I love 'em." Gracie's fervor was hard to miss.

"But a puppy isn't what you want for Christmas?" Wyatt pressed.

Gracie shook her head. After a sideways look at Ellie, she leaned close to Wyatt and whispered in his ear. Ellie didn't have to hear a word to know what she said. Her guess was confirmed by Wyatt's heartfelt sigh of resignation.

Ellie sighed, too, but silently. She packaged the rest of the cookies in a box. Clearly it was time, past time, to leave.

"Thank you very much for lending us your kitchen, Wyatt." She held the box under one arm and stretched her other hand out to Gracie. "Time to go, sweetie."

Gracie flung her arms around Wyatt's neck and squeezed hard. Ellie could hardly breathe when her daughter tilted her head and flickered her eyelashes against his cheek.

"That's a butterfly kiss," she said with a giggle, then she slid off his knee.

"Thank you, Gracie." He walked them to the door and said, "Good night," in a soft voice. His thoughtful gaze slid from her to Ellie. "Sweet dreams," he murmured.

Ellie fluttered a hand, unable to say anything

in the intimacy of the moonlight. She was too aware of Wyatt standing on the step, watching as she drove away.

"He's nice, isn't he, Mommy?"

Nice? What an insipid word to describe such a dynamic man.

"Mommy?"

Though Ellie nodded her agreement with Gracie's sentiment she privately thought the Grant women were entirely too smitten with Wyatt Wright.

"Glad you could come over, Wyatt." Tanner looked up from the tack he was sorting. "We'll sure be glad to have your help with those boys again this afternoon."

"No problem." Wyatt felt reluctant at the thought of working again with Albert, the kid Ellie was so worried about. Yet he couldn't very well refuse to help when Tanner had phoned today.

So far this one ranch was keeping his office afloat, but Wyatt's practice was a long way from the shining business his father had wished for.

"I should have asked you earlier," Tanner said with an apologetic look. "Would you be willing to have a reference check done? I'm required to get them for anyone at Wranglers Ranch who works with the kids."

"No problem. When Taryn did some design work for a government building a few years ago she made friends with a social worker who persuaded us to take the foster parent training so we could be emergency foster parents." Wyatt remembered the time fondly. "We took the whole course."

"I didn't know that." Tanner grinned. "I'm guessing they didn't teach potty training."

"I wish." Wyatt grimaced. "Cade's about ready for that, I suppose." He shuddered at the thought of training his headstrong son. "I think that's when Taryn decided she wanted a baby. It was funny, because up until then she never talked a lot about kids; but after we had those kids to stay, she couldn't talk about anything else but having her own and raising them on the ranch." He sobered suddenly, remembering that she would never mother Cade. "Anyway, the agency did a check on us back then. It's probably still in police files."

"Thanks, Wyatt," Tanner said quietly.

He shrugged. "No biggie. I'm going to take a quick look at that lame pony before your kids get here. If you still intend to use her for the Make-a-Wish ride, we can't wait for the swelling to go down by itself."

Wyatt left the tack room and headed for the pasture where the pony stood munching on hay.

He completed his examination and was returning to the house when he saw Ellie speaking to Albert. The boy looked uncomfortable. Figuring Ellie might need help, Wyatt veered their way.

"Albert," he said, nodding at the boy, who wouldn't meet his gaze. "Ellie. What's up?"

"I was just telling Albert I'd be in his neighborhood this weekend, and I wondered if he'd like to go for a soda or some ice cream with Gracie and me."

Ellie was trying hard to carry off nonchalance, but Wyatt heard the intensity behind her words. She was worried about Albert. Whether his concern was unfounded or not, he wasn't about to let Ellie go alone.

"Cade and I could use an outing. Can we come along?" he asked. "In fact, why don't we make it lunch? I'll spring for burgers."

"Do you like burgers, Albert?" Ellie asked.

"I used to love my grandmother's burgers." Albert suddenly fell silent.

"A grandmother's food is always special." Ellie smiled that sweet, gentle look that coaxed confidences. "I'd love to meet her."

"She died." Albert turned and walked away.

Ellie started toward him, but Wyatt held her arm.

"Let him go," he said softly. "He's embarrassed for you to see him cry."

"How do you know?" Ellie stared at him, her forehead pleated in a dark look.

"I was a kid his age once. I remember what it was like." Wyatt didn't want to go into the past, but he'd said too much.

"It's hardly the same. You had your home and your dad."

"Yeah." *Let it go, Ellie.*

"Tanner's beckoning." Ellie walked by his side silently for a moment, then asked, "Did you ever find out about your mother?"

"No. I did ask some of my dad's friends, but they didn't seem to know anything. Guess I'll never know now." He'd told himself a hundred times that it didn't matter, but it did. The lack of knowledge about her was like a bruised bone that wouldn't heal. It just kept aching and aching.

"I think you should hire someone to find the truth. Then you'd know." Ellie studied him for a moment, then shrugged. "Of course, maybe you'd rather not find out about her."

"Why would you think that?" Stunned by the comment, he stared at her.

"Well, it seems like you're not putting much effort into finding her." Ellie held up her hands, palms facing him. "Sorry. It's none of my business."

But she had a point. He should discover what he could and then finally put the matter to rest.

He made up his mind then and there to contact a private detective. Maybe he wouldn't like what he learned, but wasn't that better than not knowing? Besides, he owed it to Cade to learn their entire family history.

Ellie had a point on another subject, too. Forgiveness for Ted. Her words had troubled Wyatt ever since she'd said them. *God has forgiven us for so much. How can we not forgive others?* He needed to be forgiven for so many mistakes he'd made.

But Wyatt couldn't dwell on that now, because Tanner again assigned him and Ellie to work with Albert and another boy, Jason. Ellie's knowledge of horses and riding surprised Wyatt until he recalled that she'd been raised on a farm. Several times she left him alone with the two boys to treat superficial scrapes of other guests. While Jason seemed comfortable with riding, Albert acted nervous about controlling his horse.

"Jonah here wants to know what you expect of him," Wyatt explained. "He's been broken to ride, so if you don't tell him what he's supposed to do, it makes him feel like he's doing something wrong. You have to pull on the reins to get him to respond."

"But it might hurt him," Albert worried. "That thing in his mouth will cut him."

"No, the bit is for Jonah's protection. It helps

him understand what you want him to do." Wyatt strove to reassure him, relieved that Lefty had taken over with Jason. "Climb on and try again," he urged Albert. "Remember, Jonah's trying to do what you want."

As he encouraged Albert to pay attention to his horse, he couldn't help but wonder what the kid had done to end up in this program. A kid who was so worried about hurting his horse and spoke with obvious love about his grandmother hardly seemed the troubled-teen type.

A short time later Tanner called a halt to the trail ride, and Wyatt was more than ready for a coffee break. As the kids devoured the snack Sophie had prepared, Wyatt cradled his coffee and thought about how he could adapt the equipment for the Make-A-Wish child whose file Tanner had given him that morning.

"Cookie for your thoughts?" Ellie sat down beside him and handed him a huge oatmeal cookie.

"Not sure they're worth it, but thanks." He munched on the treat, suddenly very aware of the strong bond forming between him and Wranglers Ranch's nurse.

"What were you frowning about?"

"The Make-A-Wish thing." He shook his head. "I can't figure out how we can manage for that little girl they added at the last minute."

"Esther." Ellie sighed. "I know. I've been struggling with the same issue, but I just can't bring myself to say no. There has to be a way for her to ride, doesn't there? This might be the last time she's well enough to live her dream."

That's what Wyatt liked so much about Ellie Grant. Giving up wasn't even in her vocabulary, especially not when it came to kids.

"Wyatt?" She nudged him back to the present with her elbow.

He looked up to see Albert standing in front of them, looking uncomfortable. "Hey, Albert. Good work today."

"Thanks." The boy exhaled as if he was about to take a giant leap of faith, then looked straight at Ellie. "I was thinking. About the weekend. I maybe could go for an ice cream with you. If you still want to."

"Oh, I still want to, Albert," Ellie assured him.

He nodded when the bus driver called him to come. "Uh, thanks. Thanks a lot."

"See you Saturday." Ellie watched him leave, but when the bus had driven away she thumped the table with her fist. Wyatt blinked and saw the glitter of tears on her lashes.

"Hey, what's wrong?"

"Didn't you notice the marks around his wrist?" she asked, her eyes glinting with anger. "They're new, so the abuse or bullying or whatever it is hasn't stopped. But it will. I'm going to make sure of that."

"Okay, then, so we'll take Albert out for lunch on Saturday," Wyatt said mildly. "I'll pick you up when?"

"You're really coming?"

"There is no way you're going alone. And Tanner agrees with me." Wyatt thought Ellie would argue, but she didn't. Instead she exhaled a sigh of relief.

"Oh. Good. I was hating the idea of going by myself."

"But you would have, wouldn't you?" he said, knowing the answer. "He matters that much to you?"

"Every kid matters, Wyatt." Ellie sipped her coffee. "I couldn't forgive myself if something happened to Albert because I was too scared to act."

"Ellie Grant, you are, quite simply, amazing."

"No, I'm not. I'm just a mom who doesn't want a kid to get hurt." Her cheeks were flushed as red as he'd ever seen them.

"You're a great big softie." He rose and held out a hand. "Come with me."

Ellie frowned but finally placed her hand in his, allowing him to draw her up. "Where?"

"To the ponies. I need your opinion about something. And Gracie's help."

"Gracie?" Ellie walked beside him, obviously curious, but after a couple of steps she drew her hand away.

Wyatt wished she hadn't. He liked holding Ellie's hand, sharing things with her. He'd never known anyone with such a big heart. And Gracie had grown on him, too. She yearned for a father to love her in the same heart-aching way he'd yearned for his father to love him.

Be careful. You can't get too close. You can't afford to fail another woman. Your job is to father Cade, remember?

His guilt wouldn't let him forget. But as he explained his idea to modify the saddle and harness to Ellie and then Gracie when she arrived, Wyatt realized Gracie didn't care about his failures or shortcomings. All she wanted was a daddy who would love her. And he intended to do that, but as her friend. Somehow he'd have to make her understand he couldn't be more than that.

Chapter Nine

"So you've brought over some of Tanner's rescued horses." On Saturday morning Ellie studied the scruffy-looking animals surrounding Wyatt inside his pasture and thought how happy he looked among them. "To stay?"

"Temporarily. I know they're not the most handsome beasts, yet," he said. "But with some pampering, they soon will be." He smoothed his palm over the withers of the nearest stallion who quivered under his touch. "You'll be amazed by what they look like in a month."

"I don't understand why you're spending so much time worrying about your practice." Ellie smiled as he fondled the ears of a mare who bore obvious signs of malnourishment. "Caring for animals is obviously what you love most about being a vet, so why won't you accept Tanner's offer of full-time employment?"

"You wouldn't understand." He opened the gate and left the paddock, his face mirroring his inner struggle.

"Try me." She walked with him toward the house, enjoying Cade's laughter as they swung him between them with Gracie egging them on.

"I told you. Growing my practice, making it the best in the city, that was the last thing I promised my father before he died." He stopped and stared into the distance. "I promised that I'd make him proud, Ellie. That's a promise I cannot break."

"You don't think just being who you are would make him proud?" Cade tugged his hands free, then headed for the sandbox. She nodded when Gracie asked to join him.

Ellie walked with Wyatt to the patio table and sat while he poured them each a glass of lemonade. She lifted her face into the sun, loving the warm caress of it, especially after hearing numerous reports of a blizzard in North Dakota. Today she did not miss the cold or the snow that were part of her childhood, but, oh, she missed her family.

She frowned at Wyatt's smartly pressed shirt and perfectly fitting jeans, then glanced at herself. She'd chosen to dress down for the visit to Albert, choosing worn jeans, a plain shirt and her favorite battered sandals in hopes that she wouldn't stand out against Albert's usually threadbare clothes. But Wyatt's appearance gave her second thoughts. Either the man didn't own a pair of tattered jeans or he'd chosen not to wear them. As usual, he looked great. And he'd shaved.

A memory of his bristled face against hers when he'd kissed her burst to life. Her skin prickled, her heart started thumping, and her brain screamed *again, again* so loudly she could barely hear the mourning doves cooing in the gravel path.

Focus, Ellie.

She cleared her throat, took a deep breath and returned to the subject at hand.

"Wyatt, you're a well-respected veterinarian who's been asked to join the staff of a thriving ranch that's doing good work in the community. What's not to be proud of?"

"Working at Wranglers—that's not the kind of thing Dad would have admired." His face stiffened into a mask that warned her not to press any further. "He was more into status and wealth."

"Okay, but you're not your father."

"No, I definitely am not." Wyatt's emphatic response enhanced her curiosity about his troubled relationship with his father.

"So you have to do what fulfills *you*." Ellie whispered a silent prayer for a way to help him.

"I made a deathbed promise to my father, Ellie. I can't just break it. Remember the verse that says to honor your parents?"

"But you've done that. You've tried to make your business what he wanted." She sensed this part was very important to clearly state. "You honored your father as best you could when he was alive, right?"

"Well, yes…" His voice trailed away.

"Think about this." Ellie searched for the most appropriate words to help him reevaluate. "Is continuing to handle all the minutiae of running an office because of a sense of duty to your father—who is no longer here to see it, I might add—how you really want to fill your life?"

"I'd rather work with animals than do books or send out bills any day. Who wouldn't?" His quick response showed that he'd asked himself the question before. The way Wyatt now plunged a hand through his hair revealed his confusion with the answer. That rumpled hair also added immensely to his good looks. "But I did make the promise."

"That was what—ten years ago?" Ellie made a face. "Isn't it time for a new perspective?"

"What perspective?" He looked at her, his brow puckered.

"You are an amazing vet, Wyatt." Ellie drew a deep breath of courage, then leaned forward until her face was mere inches from his, determined to make him see what she saw. "You love working with animals, and it shows every time you handle one."

"Thank you." Her flattery embarrassed him, but Ellie would have none of that.

"Don't thank me because it's true. Animal medicine is your God-given gift." An idea formed. "Have you ever read that sign Tanner has hanging above the door of the barn?"

"'Fan into flame the gift that is within you,'" he recited with a nod.

"Right. So if God has given you such an incredible gift with animals, isn't your job to fan it, as in to do the most with that gift that you can?" She let the question hang for a moment.

"It's not that easy, Ellie."

"Isn't it?" She loved the way he kept his focus on her when she spoke to him, as if at this moment she and what she had to say were the most important things in his world. "As I see it there's only one question to ask, and you must answer honestly."

"I'll try," he promised.

"So the 64,000-dollar question is this—where does your heart lie? In building your own practice into the biggest in Tucson or in working directly with the animals?" Ellie waited for him to think it through.

"When you put it like that—" He sighed. "It doesn't help."

"There's another verse in the Bible that might. Ecclesiastes 9, verse 10 says, 'Whatever your hand finds to do, do it with your might.'"

"Interesting." He nodded, but she knew he was wondering where this was headed.

"Whenever I see you working with the animals I think of that verse," Ellie admitted.

"Why?" Wyatt blinked in confusion.

"Because you never settle for half measures. You put your whole heart into treating an animal. You don't doubt what you're doing or second-guess your decisions. You especially don't consider whether or not you'll make someone proud." She heard the fervor in her voice but couldn't stem it. "You treat needy animals because you can't bear to see them suffer when you can stop it, and because it's what you love to do. Because that's where your heart is. Correct?"

"I guess." He shrugged.

"So tell me, Wyatt." She met his stare unflinchingly. "Can you put that same devotion, that same pride and compassion into making your practice the biggest one in Tucson?"

"I don't know." He fell into thought, only speaking again after several moments had passed. "Yes, I enjoy working at Wranglers Ranch. I especially enjoy having Tanner as a spiritual mentor." He winked. "And I'm enjoying Gracie's stubbornly determined spirit more every day. She doesn't give up on us no matter how often we use her as a guinea pig to figure out preparations for the Make-a-Wish kids."

"You're digressing," Ellie pointed out.

"Yes, a bit," he admitted. "I need time to think things through. But about Gracie—she's so willing to help. It's a great quality in anyone but especially nice in a kid."

"I notice you left me out of that admiration society." Ellie felt the sting deep inside and chided herself for it. Why did Wyatt's opinion of her matter so much?

"Not true. In fact, you're at the top of my People-I-Most-Appreciate list." Wyatt's eyes twinkled. "I like how you challenge me to do more with my faith, Ellie."

"Ah, you're talking about this morning and how I roped you into helping with the church kids' Christmas program."

He nodded, not even pretending to hide his grin.

"Well, you did agree to meet me at the church," she defended. "And since you were there already, who else would I bug about figuring out how to get their angel to hover over the manger?"

"Yeah," he said with a chuckle. "You go with that excuse." His face grew pensive as he swirled his lemonade before taking a drink. "But actually I meant how you challenged me to forgive Ted."

"I challenged you? How?"

"I forget your exact words." Wyatt stared directly at her. "The part that lodged in my brain was that if I expect God's forgiveness for the messes I've made in my life, I owe others some forgiveness, too."

"I don't think I said anything of the kind, but it is a precept that's worth remembering. 'Do unto others,' right?" Ellie had a hunch that if he could break free of the blame, he'd find it much easier to move ahead with his life. "The one thing I too often forget is that God loves us, warts and all. He sees into the depths of our hearts, knows our worst secret and loves us in spite of it."

"I have a lot to be forgiven for," Wyatt mumbled.

"I believe we all do." She liked his humility so much.

"You don't understand." He sighed. "I wish I could undo the past. I made so many mistakes in my marriage, broke so many promises to Taryn."

Wyatt's admission forced the realization that she'd never had this kind of conversation with Eddie. He'd never been this open with her about his past or his mistakes. In fact, he'd hated to discuss anything truly personal. Further proof that their marriage could not have worked. *Thank You, God that You saved me from that failure.*

Wyatt wasn't like Eddie, but it was now clearer than ever that, despite her feelings for him, there could be nothing between them. God had given her the job of raising Gracie. The older her daughter got, the more attention and love she would need. Ellie couldn't get sidetracked by her own wants. Often God called people to sacrifice, especially moms. Wincing at the pain of that, she tuned back in to what Wyatt was saying.

"I never loved my father the way I should have." His chin rested on his chest, his lowered voice revealing his shame. "I still feel like I failed him. I'm sure not the best parent for Cade. I make mistakes, get frustrated..."

"Wyatt." She placed her hand on his arm to draw his attention, cherishing the intimacy of these confidences he shared with her. When he lifted his head to look at her with his deep, dark gaze she smiled. "Welcome to the human race."

He rolled his eyes.

"I'm serious. I haven't been a Christian for very long, and there's much I have to learn," Ellie admitted. "But the one thing Sophie *has* drummed into me is that none of us is perfect, but God loves us anyway, and the important thing is that we keep trying to do His will."

"And forgiving Ted is His will." He nodded.

"Got it. So that's not in question. What is in question is whether or not I can do it." He stared at Cade. "Every time I think about Ted, I get furious. He took Cade's mother. How do I forgive that, Ellie?"

There was so much pain in Wyatt's face that it took Ellie's breath away. She longed to wrap her arms around him and comfort him. But she couldn't do that. Wyatt had made it clear long ago that he did not want a romantic relationship. And neither did she, despite the overwhelming attraction she felt for him. Yet she had to help him. Somehow.

"No answers?" he said, managing a weak smile.

"I don't know how you find forgiveness, Wyatt," she admitted. "But God does. I think you'll have to ask Him to show you, because I'm pretty sure forgiveness is your only way out of the pain."

Ellie left Wyatt with his private thoughts, stepping away. She'd never known anyone like him, and she wanted to know more. In that moment she regretted her promise to Albert. Of course she still wanted to see where the boy lived and with whom, only not today. Not now when Wyatt was finally opening up to her. If only…

"I guess we'd better get going." Wyatt rose, collected their glasses and carried them inside.

A few moments later he returned with a light jacket for Cade.

He walked over and swung the boy into his arms, gently shaking him to free the excess sand from his clothes. "I probably should bathe him."

"Why bother?" Ellie called Gracie to come. "You're the only one who looks model-perfect. Besides, I have some wipes." With her hand midway into her backpack to reach for the package, she stopped at his shout of laughter.

"Of course you do," Wyatt guffawed. "Shades of other messy meetings." He winked at her, then held out a hand. "Okay, give me some and let's mop 'em up."

He made cleaning the children's hands and faces into a game, and by the time they were finished, both Gracie and Cade were giggling. On that happy note they set out for the address Albert had given them.

"It's a rough-looking section of town," Wyatt muttered as they searched for the right house number. "I don't like the way those two guys on the corner are watching us."

Neither did Ellie, but there was nothing to do but keep going.

"There's Albert." Ellie waved at him. When Wyatt had parked, she opened her door and climbed out of the truck. "Hi. Ready to go?"

"I guess." The boy glanced behind him hesitantly, then left the front step to walk toward them.

"I tried to call and ask permission from your mom for you to come with us, but I couldn't get an answer at the number you gave me. Is there someone else I should speak to?" Ellie noted the curtain twitch in the front window.

"My mom doesn't live here." Albert climbed into the truck. "This is my uncle's place."

Ellie was about to say she'd ask his permission, but Albert assured her that it was fine for him to go and that no one but his older cousin was at home anyway.

"Your cousin knows you'll be with us?" After Albert nodded Ellie debated a moment longer, then gave up when Wyatt urged her to get into the truck.

But as they drove toward the restaurant, Ellie had second thoughts. She should have put this outing off until she'd been able to contact Albert's guardian. But her need to know, to help him or at least get him away for a time, had overtaken good sense. All she could do now was apologize to whomever was at his house when they returned and hope the person she believed was maltreating him realized that she and Wyatt were looking out for Albert.

Within minutes they were seated in a booth in

the restaurant. Gracie soon had their guest talking freely and laughing at Cade's antics. They all ordered, except for Albert who wouldn't choose anything.

"I don't need to eat," he kept saying, though it was obvious from his rapt attention to other guests' meals that he was hungry.

"It's been a while since breakfast time, right?" Wyatt guessed. "Order another, or lunch if you'd rather. I had kind of a late start to the day and missed my breakfast so I'm famished."

"So am I." Ellie grinned at him, enjoying the camaraderie.

"I didn't know you were married," Albert said, his glance moving back and forth between them.

"We're not married!" Too aware of Wyatt's shoulder rubbing hers, Ellie shifted away, then felt suddenly bereft of the contact. Why had she chosen this booth instead of a roomy table where they wouldn't have to sit so close? "I drove out to Wyatt's ranch this morning so we could come together in his truck because my car is too small for all of us. Now what will you have to eat?"

Gracie finally persuaded Albert to match her pancake order.

All during the meal Ellie used every tactic she could think of to coax Albert to talk about himself, but he offered little response. Only with

Gracie and Cade did he seem perfectly comfortable, again mentioning his late grandmother.

Ellie reached across to pat his hand. "It's good you had some family you could come to." She'd said that deliberately, ignoring Wyatt's nudge under the table while she watched Albert, trying to gauge his reaction.

"I guess." Albert didn't look at her, and Ellie grew more worried.

"I thought after breakfast we might take a drive out to the Sonoran Desert Museum." Wyatt wiped the sticky pancake syrup off Cade's face. "I haven't been there in a while. I wouldn't mind seeing the raptor flights again."

"Would you like to go, Albert?" Ellie asked.

"Doesn't matter to me," he said, showing no emotion.

"Maybe we should stop by your place and make sure it's okay with your uncle," Wyatt offered with a meaningful glance at Ellie.

"He won't care."

It wasn't the words; it was the way Albert said them that bothered Ellie. As if it didn't matter to him that his own uncle didn't care where Albert went or what he did.

"I'll try calling him again." Ellie pulled out her phone and dialed, but there was no response. "I guess there's still no one home."

Did Albert look relieved? She wasn't sure. She

kept close watch on him as they walked the paths at the Desert Museum, noting his interest in the animal displays, especially the javelina pigs.

"Okay, let's keep going," Wyatt urged after a prolonged viewing. "There's a lot more to see."

Ellie wondered how silly and schoolgirlish it was to like the way he kept them together, to enjoy his hand on her back as he shepherded her past some youths that were roughhousing. Was it wrong to revel in his arm looping through hers and tugging her in a different direction than she'd intended? Well, if it was, so be it. Because Ellie was delighting in this day more with every passing moment.

Until she read the sign that said what lay ahead.

"Reptiles?" she hissed in Wyatt's ear, squeezing his arm.

"Of course." He flashed her his Hollywood smile. "That's my favorite exhibit. Why?"

"Oh, no reason." She forced her fingers to unclench and waged combat on every nerve that screamed *no way.*

In the dim underground display where the others ogled reptiles wriggling and writhing, the truth crawled up Ellie's skittering nerves and smacked her in the heart.

She was willing to be here, even to endure snakes, to be with Wyatt Wright.

Because she was in love with him?

* * *

Wyatt wasn't exactly sure where or when it happened, but somewhere along the way the fun of their trip to the Desert Museum lost its enjoyment for Ellie.

No matter how he explained the features of the different animals, he couldn't hold Ellie's attention. Albert and Gracie were avid pupils while he enthused about toads, turtles and tree frogs, but when they neared the rattlesnake display he noted Ellie shy away, keeping a good distance between herself and the glass.

Because she was terrified, he suddenly realized and wished he'd noted her aversion earlier. What a good sport she was to stay there and let everyone else appreciate what she hated. He wanted her to have fun today. He had to do something.

"I'm thirsty," he announced. "Let's go to the restaurant. Ellie?"

Stirring as if from a fog she nodded. "C-coffee sounds g-good," she stammered and immediately headed for the exit.

Wyatt felt a tug on his pant leg and glanced down. Gracie motioned to him to bend over.

"Mommy doesn't like snakes," she whispered in his ear. "But don't tell her I tol' you. 'Kay?"

"Our secret," Wyatt agreed and glanced at Albert, who nodded.

"Girls are usually scared of snakes," the boy said as if he possessed much worldly knowledge about the female of the species.

Wyatt hid a grin as he followed them out. He found Ellie waiting far down the path, as if she couldn't get enough distance between herself and the reptile enclosure.

"Albert was just telling me that girls often don't like snakes," he said to Ellie. He winked at Albert. "Was your grandmother one of those girls?"

"Yeah. Gran hated snakes." A smile lit up Albert's thin face. Was this the first time the boy had been able to share his memories of that woman? "If Gran thought there was a snake nearby, she'd get out this big old garden boot, and she wouldn't let go of it until the snake was dead or gone. She even took that boot to bed once. Kept it on the pillow right next to her head."

Gracie hooted with laughter. Wyatt joined in. Even Cade gurgled with amusement. Only Ellie seemed to think such an action was perfectly logical.

As they walked up the path to the café, Gracie pestered Albert for more stories about his grandmother, and Albert obliged, apparently enjoying sharing his memories, especially about her cooking.

The restaurant was very busy so Wyatt suggested they quickly choose a table on the deck outside before everything was filled up.

"Sitting in the shade up here and savoring this amazing view of the valley is the perfect accompaniment to iced coffee." Wyatt handed Ellie Cade. "What would the rest of you like?"

"Iced tea for me, please." Ellie tickled Cade. "Maybe milk for this guy?"

"Ice cream?" Gracie asked Ellie.

Ellie wrinkled her nose. "Milk?" she suggested. Cade swung his arms wildly, as if to disagree.

"Ice cream's like milk," Albert said thoughtfully. "Only thicker and colder."

"An' lots better to eat," Gracie agreed. She turned to Wyatt. "Me an' Albert an' Cade would like ice cream, please."

She did not, Wyatt noted as he hid a smile, check with her mother. But when Cade started bellowing as if he agreed with Gracie he howled with laughter. After a moment Ellie joined in. Her lovely musical laugh echoed across the balcony, turning many heads. He knew exactly what the people who studied them were thinking; here was a family truly enjoying their day at the museum.

And for some strange reason Wyatt didn't mind them thinking that. Because, in some weird kind of way, maybe they were—a family of stragglers who'd banded together to have some fun. That's what Ellie did, he realized. She brought people together and helped them laugh.

That's exactly what she'd done for him.

While Ellie stayed at the table with Cade, Wyatt took Gracie and Albert inside to help carry the ice cream. While they waited he glanced out the window and found he couldn't look away from the vision of Ellie playing with his son. She was so pretty, a real natural at motherhood with her generous, nurturing spirit. Ellie was the kind of woman most men dreamed of having for a wife.

Whoa!

Wyatt forcibly reined in his thoughts. Forgiving Ted, that made sense. He needed to get past that hurdle to fully live his Christian faith.

But starting another relationship, even with someone as great as Ellie, was something Wyatt could not allow himself to consider. Too many broken promises blocked that path, too many memories of how he'd failed.

So for the rest of the afternoon Wyatt worked hard to stop the myriad images of Ellie from engraving in his head. And failed. Ellie laughing as she tried to photograph a darting roadrunner, smiling when a bee kept buzzing Wyatt, teasing Cade out of his grumpiness and making everyone's day a little happier. His brain captured and stored a thousand images of sweet, generous, earnest Ellie.

After they'd shared a barbecue dinner at his ranch, after they'd driven Albert home and Ellie had left, after he'd put Cade to bed, poured himself a fresh lemonade and sat on his patio—when the world had fallen silent around him—Wyatt let those images play like a recording that he couldn't erase. Didn't want to.

Because Ellie Grant was a very special woman.

Chapter Ten

"He said what?" Ellie couldn't believe the words she just heard. Maybe she was in a Monday morning fog.

"This morning Wyatt told Tanner he accepted his offer of full-time employment at Wranglers Ranch." Sophie hugged her in a burst of exuberance. "Isn't it wonderful? A true answer to our prayers."

"Wonderful," Ellie repeated, feeling dazed. When Sophie left she passed the morning preparing for Albert's group to visit this afternoon while her mind repeated one question. What in the world had happened to change Wyatt's mind about breaking the promise to his father?

She'd seen him at church yesterday, and he hadn't said a word. She'd sat beside him at the Christmas potluck afterward, and he hadn't mentioned closing his office. She'd gone back to his ranch to do another batch of baking yesterday afternoon, with Albert lending a hand decorating the cookies, and still Wyatt hadn't said anything. Though she repeatedly searched her brain, Ellie found nothing to suggest that Wyatt had been considering this action.

She had tons of questions to ask the handsome veterinarian, but Wyatt never appeared.

"He asked for the morning off to make some phone calls about his practice." Tanner answered her question about his whereabouts when she joined him and Sophie for lunch on the patio. "He'll be here for the class after lunch."

"What about Cade?" She blushed at Tanner and Sophie's shared glances of amusement.

"Cade will have a sitter every morning and every other afternoon. If I have to call Wyatt in, I told him to bring Cade along, and we'd figure out something." He kept a straight face as he asked, "Is there a problem if I ask you to care for him?"

"Of course not."

"Truth be told, you'd relish the opportunity to hold that little guy in your arms again, wouldn't you?" Sophie teased.

"So I like kids." Ellie concentrated on eating.

"Cade's a cutie, all right." Tanner swallowed the last of his coffee and rose. "Say, did you ever get to speak to Albert's uncle?"

"No." Ellie frowned. "His house looked dark when we dropped Albert off last night, as if no one was home. But he insisted his cousin would be around, and I had to get Gracie home—"

"You don't have to apologize, Ellie. It's not your job, or Wyatt's, to care for Albert, but it does raise some questions about the folks whose job it is." Tanner kissed Sophie goodbye. "I'll be sorting out tack," he said, giving her a long look, as if he couldn't bear to be far from her side.

Ellie's heart ached for someone to look at her with that same gaze of adoration. But that was silly to hope for when she knew what God expected. With a sigh she buried herself in her work until she heard the bus rolling in. Then she pasted a smile on her face and went out to greet the kids.

She managed to keep her mind off Wyatt while the boys demonstrated their ability to curry their animals. Then they were learning how to trot their mounts when Wyatt appeared on the other side of Albert's horse. Ellie couldn't control her racing heart or the silly smile she knew she wore.

"I hear you'll be joining our staff. Welcome." She pretended her smile was purely professional. "I think you'll enjoy it here."

"News travels fast." He stopped Albert to

point out his loose cinch, then grinned at her. "I already enjoy it here."

"Good." *Don't read anything into his friendliness, Ellie. He's one of the nice guys—to everyone.*

"I took more of your advice last night." He offered his encouragement as Albert tightened the cinch, then nervously climbed on the horse and nudged it to move.

"My advice?" Ellie gulped when Wyatt swiveled to look at her. "What was that?"

Wyatt leaned forward and whispered, "I asked God to help me forgive Ted."

"Great." She noticed the way he glanced around at the group and saw how the corners of his mouth tightened.

"I think that's going to take some doing, though, because as I look around, I don't feel compassion for most of these kids."

"You need a different filter." Ellie grinned. "It's something Pastor Jeff said in his sermon a few weeks ago. When it's hard for us to do as God instructs us, Jeff suggested we put on a 'God filter' that strips away all the things we see as so good about ourselves and see what God sees."

"Which is?"

"The view that we are no better than the next

guy, that we need forgiveness just as much as he does, and maybe more."

There was no time to talk for the rest of the lesson as Ellie was called on to treat a boy who'd caught his foot in a stirrup when dismounting. But that didn't stop her from silently praying for Wyatt as she worked.

She escorted the boy to the gate and remained, smiling and waving as the kids loaded onto the bus. Albert had a window seat, and after a moment's hesitation, he waved back at her, his smile faint but still there.

When the group was gone, the staff gathered for a coffee break on the patio where Tanner made a little speech welcoming Wyatt to their group. Ellie forced herself to keep her applause mild, but inside she was jumping with joy because she'd now see Wyatt almost every day.

Foolish, her brain chided. She wanted to ignore it, but Gracie's arrival off the bus reminded her of her duty.

Ellie was more than ready to put some distance between herself and the ranch so she could sort out her feelings for Wyatt. But her daughter, it seemed, was not.

"We hafta go to Cade's place," Gracie said as she tossed her backpack into the car.

"Oh, honey, not tonight. I've got so much to do to get ready for Christmas." Ellie knew from the jut of Gracie's chin that reason wasn't going to work. "Why do you need to go there?"

"I hafta do something Melissa said to do 'bout my gift for Cade." Gracie frowned darkly. "An' I can't tell you what 'cause it's a secret."

"What's a secret?" Wyatt asked after stepping out from a stand of sycamores. He listened carefully to what Gracie said, wrinkled his nose and shot Ellie a questioning look.

"She won't tell me." Ellie shrugged, wishing she could control the rush of joy that filled her every time he appeared.

"I don't think today is a very good time, Gracie."

Something about Wyatt's voice got Ellie's attention. She surreptitiously studied him, wondering what had happened to turn his eyes so dark and turbulent.

"Oh." Gracie deflated. There was no other description to fully convey the way her chest slumped, her shoulders dipped, and her lips drooped. "But Christmas isn't very far away," she pleaded.

"Exactly nine days," Ellie added almost but not quite under her breath.

"And you've got things to do." Wyatt nodded. "So do I. Maybe another time, Gracie." He turned to walk away. To Ellie's eyes he also looked deflated. And maybe a little cross?

"You stay here, honey," she ordered Gracie. "I need to talk to Wyatt in private."

"Please, Mommy, please get him to let us come. Please?" Gracie begged, hope sparkling in her blue eyes just the way Karen's had when she and Ellie were young.

"I don't think so. Now, stay here," she directed.

"An' pray. That's what I'll do." Gracie flopped down on a stump and clasped her hands.

Shaking her head, Ellie walked up to Wyatt. "Is something wrong? You seem—"

She wasn't prepared when he whirled to face her, fury evident in his body language.

"He's coming here."

"Who?" Ellie had never seen him this angry.

"Ted." He glared at the phone he still held in his hand. "I just had a phone call from a friend who learned that Ted was never charged with Taryn's accident."

"I'm so sorry." She knew how much he'd been counting on Ted's punishment to make him feel that his wife's needless death would be avenged.

"That's not the worst of it." Wyatt's jaw flexed. "Apparently he has some youth sponsor from the church, a do-gooder who wants to be sure that poor Ted doesn't suffer any negative effects from his brush with the law, so he's enrolled him in a program here, at Wranglers.

Isn't that rich? Ted gets to ride horses while Cade goes without his mother."

"I don't know what to say." Ellie could hardly stand to watch his pain. "I'm so sorry you have to go through this."

"I don't have to." His jaw clenched again as he turned to peer into the brush. "I'm going to resign. I should never have taken the job here anyway."

"But you don't have clients." Suddenly she knew not seeing Wyatt every day would be far worse than enduring the pain of seeing him, loving him and not being able to do anything about it. "You can't quit."

"I can't be here when he comes, can't watch him gloating over his escape from justice," he said in a cracked voice.

"Oh, Wyatt." Ellie couldn't help it. She stepped forward and drew him into her arms, hurting because he hurt and desperate to assuage his pain.

As Wyatt's arms slid around her waist and he drew her near, his breath brushed her ear. For a moment it was pure bliss to be so close, to be the one he leaned on, the one he turned to for support. But even as those thoughts filled her head, Ellie knew it couldn't last.

So she eased away, breaking contact with him, though it was so hard not to let that embrace go on and on. But that wasn't what either of them needed right now.

"Tell me what you're thinking," she urged.

"That I let myself get too consumed with work and Cade. I keep making the same old mistake over and over." A sigh came from deep within him. "I should have done something, insisted the police find more evidence. Something, anything, because now Ted's going to get away with what he did."

"Wait a minute." Ellie squeezed her eyes closed to think. When she opened them Wyatt was staring at her, a frown on his face. "Who said Ted did anything wrong?"

"The police?" Wyatt's confusion was obvious. "He was arrested. He was found at the scene. I don't know what you're saying, Ellie."

"I'm saying you don't know the reason he wasn't charged." She had to get him to refocus. "You don't know anything about Ted, not for sure."

"I know what the cops told me." Wyatt stared at her as if she'd somehow betrayed him.

"That was how long ago? The night Taryn died?" she asked quietly and waited for his nod. "You lost your wife, Wyatt. You were grieving, you had a baby to care for, a funeral to plan, a life to put back together. Two lives. That was more than enough for you to handle. It was the duty of the police and the courts to find out who was to blame and to punish them."

"Which they have not done." He was clearly unable to reconcile his anger and guilt.

"How do you know?" She touched his arm, trying to make him reconsider. "You're angry and upset. All this time, since that awful night, you've blamed Ted for ruining your life. You haven't been able to forgive him, you said."

"No, but I thought that if I tried hard, if I was willing to let go of everything..." He exhaled. "But I can't."

"Can I say something?" She saw his nod but hesitated. "You won't want to hear me, Wyatt. It will hurt, and you've had a bellyful of hurt already. But I think you need to consider who you can't forgive."

His head jerked up, and he gaped at her.

"What I mean is this. You've tried so hard to do the right thing, be the right son, to not repeat your father's mistakes. And yet your life got dumped on." She touched his arm, trying to soften words that couldn't be softened. "Are you really truly unable to forgive Ted?" she whispered. "Or is it God you can't forgive for letting Taryn die, for letting your perfect family be destroyed?"

The words hung in the air. How she wished

she could take them back, could unsay them and never have to remember Wyatt's devastated eyes.

"No, Ellie. That's not it." He glared at her, his face rigid and unyielding. "Taryn died because I didn't keep my promise to her. If I had, she'd still be alive." The harsh words hit her like ice pellets. "I have to live with that. But I'm not the only one to blame. Ted should pay for his part in her death, and now he won't. That's what I can't forgive. Or forget."

Then he turned and walked off. A moment later his truck roared away from the ranch.

"He doesn't want us, does he?" Gracie stood watching the red plumes of dust with tears rolling down her cheeks. "He's got Cade and he doesn't need anybody else in his family. He doesn't want to be my daddy."

Ellie consoled her daughter all the way home, then went to extreme lengths to cheer her up by letting her try on her angel costume for the concert. But later she sent a constant barrage of prayers heavenward. Not just prayers for Gracie, but for a man, a generous, kind veterinarian caught in a maelstrom of pain, anger and bitter regret.

Please, please, don't let me love him.

What a futile prayer. Wyatt Wright was embedded in her heart.

* * *

At first Wyatt held off on giving his resignation, because he was too embarrassed to cancel on Tanner when he had such huge expectations for the Make-A-Wish kids. He went to work, did his job and pretended everything was normal. And he avoided Ellie.

If only it was so easy to avoid her voice in his head.

Is it God you can't forgive for letting Taryn die?

Somewhere in those words he thought he heard a ring of truth, but unable to handle more than his new job, his son and his needy ranch, Wyatt blocked them out in exactly the same way he blocked out the memory of Ellie holding him, trying to comfort him. Ellie the nurturer.

He was successful at avoiding her for one day. Then she tracked him to the farthest quarter of Wranglers Ranch on a horse she could barely sit.

"I have something to tell you, and you've no alternative but to listen to me." Her hair was a halo of mussed curls, her face glowed with perspiration, and she kept rubbing one hand as if it hurt. "This time you cannot run away."

"Who said I was running?" he asked, then gave up because there was absolutely no point in lying to Ellie. She homed in on truth like hummingbirds to nectar.

"Now, listen to me, Wyatt, because this is important." She dismounted then sat down on a bale, her eyes locking on him. "Albert is Ted."

"What?" He couldn't figure out what she meant.

"His real name is Albert, but his relatives call him Ted. That's the name you heard the police use that night." She studied him as if trying to assess his reaction. "Well?" she demanded, frustrated by his lack of response. "Aren't you going to say anything?"

"How do you know this?" He fiddled with his gloves, trying not to stare at her and failing. She was so lovely, especially when that temper showed.

"He came to decorate cookies last night. That's when he told Gracie that his uncle had started calling him Ted because he said he was fat like a teddy bear."

Wyatt just sat there, trying hard to make sense of what she'd said.

"Do you want to hear the rest?" she demanded.

"Do I have a choice?" He watched a pucker form on her brow and nodded. "That's what I thought. Continue."

"When he was five, Albert's mother left him with his grandmother and never came back. His Gran was a wonderful woman who loved him and raised him right. But she died and that left eleven-year-old Albert—eleven, Wyatt," she emphasized in case he hadn't heard her the first time. "It left that poor kid at the mercy of his relatives whom, I might add, have a very disreputable reputation, according to a certain social worker I know."

"Ah, the hard luck story."

Her eyes narrowed in warning.

"Sorry," he apologized, though he wasn't in the least sorry. Ellie mad was really something to see. "Go on."

She studied him with a glower that said she wasn't sure he was serious, then shifted from the bale to the ground and continued.

"Yes, I will, because you need to hear this to understand who Ted is." She blew her bangs off her forehead.

"Okay then, go on." He looked at her and realized he'd missed her. This steamrollering nurse who didn't take no for an answer, didn't even hear it, truth be told.

"So here's this orphaned kid and, despite having to change his home and school and move into that drug-infested neighborhood where his sketchy, not to mention abusive, relatives live—" Her steely gray eyes dared him to argue with that assessment. "Despite losing the only mother he's ever known, our Ted manages to steer clear of trouble and keep up his excellent grades."

"A model citizen, in fact. Bravo." He was deliberately goading her, but he couldn't stop, couldn't make himself forget what Ted had done.

"He really is, Wyatt. And you know what? He had nothing to do with your wife's death." She must have seen his skepticism. "It's the truth, and there are many witnesses who back up his story, which is why he's innocent. He was only at the scene that night because his cousin—the driver of the car—called him for help. Because he was scared and he knew Ted would know what to do. Which was good because Ted called 911."

Ellie leaned back on her hands and studied him like a hawk with prey, obviously waiting for his reaction. But Wyatt struggled to comprehend what she'd said.

"Don't you get it? Ted isn't guilty of Taryn's death." Her tone modulated. "He doesn't deserve your anger, Wyatt, and he doesn't need your forgiveness because he didn't do anything wrong."

"He was still there." The feeble excuse sounded pathetic even to him. But he'd blamed the kid for so long, blamed an innocent boy when the blame lay directly on himself.

"Let it go." Ellie shook her head. "It's not doing you any good to hang on to this ill will. Besides…"

He recognized that pause; it meant she had

something else to say, something she thought he wouldn't like.

"Besides?"

"What if the situation was different, Wyatt? What if Cade was the kid someone was blaming for something that wasn't his fault?" Those gray eyes wouldn't let him ignore the truth. "Would you want them to treat Cade as unfairly as you're treating Ted?"

Trust Ellie to illustrate his stubbornness so perfectly.

"Okay, I get it. But it's going to take me a while." He heaved a sigh because the truth could no longer be disputed no matter how unpalatable it was. "I have to mentally mesh Albert and Ted, figure out how to deal with what I thought I knew. It won't happen overnight."

"I know." She rose, walked over to him and touched his arm. "It won't be easy, but you'll do it, Wyatt."

"How do you know that?" he demanded, frustrated by the idealized vision she seemed to have of him. Couldn't she tell how unsatisfied he was by this knowledge? Couldn't she see that Albert's—Ted's—innocence only made his own guilt seem worse?

"Because of who your Father is. God will heal your heart, if you let Him." Ellie's words triggered an awareness inside him. The hole Taryn's death had left in his heart *was* healing, thanks in part to Ellie's gentle comfort but also because of Gracie's unwavering love.

But if his faith was real, if he truly believed God was the master of his life, there was more to the story.

"What are you thinking, Wyatt? Please, tell me." Ellie stood before him now, her face troubled as she waited.

"It's just dawned on me." Wyatt could hardly wrap his brain around it. "Ted—Albert—I can't blame anyone because, in truth, Taryn's life was in God's hands. That's what she believed. He's who she trusted completely."

"Yes." Ellie smiled, but she still waited expectantly.

A flicker of something fresh, something joyful seemed to come alive inside him.

"Nothing happens unless God allows it. He knew she'd die that night and that it would be my fault for breaking my promise."

"Right." A huge grin spread across her face. "He knew, and He forgives you. Don't you think Taryn would, too, if she was here?"

"Yes." He had to admit it, because she had not been one to hold grudges. "She wouldn't have liked the way I've been."

"But she would have understood." Ellie pinned him with her gaze. "If Taryn were here right now, wouldn't she encourage you to reach out to Albert, to help him however you can? Isn't that the kind of woman your wife was, Wyatt?"

"Yes." He studied Ellie, suddenly thankful that she hadn't left him in his misery, blame and unforgiveness, so glad that she'd pushed and prodded and nudged him to the truth. "I've made a lot of mistakes," he murmured. "And I'll probably make more in the future."

"Of course you will." Ellie chuckled at his dour look. "Because you're human," she added with a wink. Her eyebrows arched. "And...?"

"And I promise I'll give Albert a chance." There he was, making promises again, but somehow Wyatt thought he might be able to keep this one with God and Ellie's help.

He was not prepared for Ellie's squeal of delight or for the way she launched herself into his arms. But he liked it.

"Oh, Wyatt, I'm so glad." Ellie's arms tightened around his neck as she hugged him. "Albert needs our help and—" Suddenly the words stopped. She shifted, easing back from him, her cheeks flushed. "I'm sorry, I wasn't thinking. I know we're not either of us looking for a relationship—"

Was that true?

His arms still around her waist, Wyatt held on and let himself bask in her sudden shyness.

Holding Ellie like this—it felt right, as if she belonged there. He'd loved Taryn, but the hole her loss had left in his heart was healing now, thanks in part to Ellie's gentle nudges into the future and to Gracie's sturdy faith in God. And his heart—was Ellie in it?

"Wyatt, I should—"

"Ellie?" He cupped her silken cheek in his palm.

"Yes?" She gazed at him.

"Be quiet." Then he leaned in and kissed her.

And Ellie kissed him back.

Chapter Eleven

"My father would not have approved of all this Christmas fuss."

Ellie froze for a moment, wondering if she should offer some sort of platitude to ease the situation. She felt confused, giddy, wary and a thousand other emotions every time she was near Wyatt. Because of his kiss yesterday.

Wonderful though it had been to be enveloped in his arms, to share that tender moment with him, nothing had been the same since.

"Maybe your mom would've," Gracie said, not even glancing up from the snowman cookie she was frosting.

"Maybe she would have. I don't know." Wyatt helped Cade press another snowman out of the cookie dough, and Albert slipped it onto a baking sheet.

"Well, arn'cha gonna look for her?" Gracie demanded. "That's what I'd do if I lost my mommy."

"Smart cookie," Wyatt said, and they all shared a laugh.

"Wyatt has been looking, honey," Ellie said, and for the moment, that seemed to satisfy her daughter.

Ellie waited until Cade was asleep and she and Wyatt were having coffee on the patio while Gracie and Albert finished the cookie decorating, before she asked, "You haven't learned anything more about your mom?"

"The investigator says he has a lead he's checking out. We'll see," he said with a shrug. "Want to order a pizza for supper?"

"We could." A little thrill tiptoed across her brain at the prospect of spending more time with this amazing man. "On one condition."

"Name it." He grinned at her, and Ellie's heart flew sky high.

"That we get your Christmas tree up." Ellie wondered at his frown. "You need to celebrate Christmas, Wyatt. I don't think it's too early to teach Cade about Christ's birth."

"A tree, besides all the stuff you and Gracie have already added?" He nodded toward the house, to where she'd added pinecones on the table, homemade wreaths on the doors, paper cutouts on the windows. He grinned, though she saw several emotions skitter across his expressive face. Finally, he nodded. "Okay, we'll go get a tree as soon as Cade wakes up."

And that was how the five of them ended up eating pizza at the mall before they loaded up on ornaments and lights.

"Uh, do you know what excessive means?" Ellie asked as they stood in line at a checkout.

"You mean as in wasting an inordinate amount of money on glittery geegaws that will be garbage by next year?" He nodded. "Yes, I do know what excessive means, Ellie."

The way he said it, in a mocking tone, told her that someone had once said those very words to him and that the memory was not a pleasant one. Ellie was guessing that person had been his father and that the teeming shopping cart in front of Wyatt was his way of exorcising the negatives of his youth.

"Oh, good." She grinned at him. "Albert, could you get another package of lights? One can never have too many lights."

Albert glanced from her to Wyatt, shrugged and left with Gracie in tow.

"Clearly that kid knows about excessive," Wyatt muttered. "Too bad nobody ever showered him with it."

"Maybe we can be the first," Ellie said.

"What do you mean?" Wyatt said.

"Ever heard of Christmas gifts?"

He groaned. "Another reason to shop?"

"Why not, when we're using your credit card?" Ellie couldn't stop her giggle.

"My father did not approve of credit cards," he said when they were on their way to his truck with the bulging cart.

"What did he approve of?" Ellie asked, only half serious.

"Not much. Not me, for sure."

"I'm sure that's not true. I'm sure he loved you in his own way." Except she wasn't sure. And now she'd begun wondering if the parenting worries she'd once heard Wyatt mention stemmed from fear that he'd somehow lose Cade's love as he'd lost his father's.

"We didn't get a tree," Ellie suddenly realized as they left the mall.

"We will. I know exactly the tree I want." Wyatt leaned forward, peering through the windshield as he drove. "It used to be right along… Yeah, here it is." He turned into a nursery lot that glowed with so much Christmas decor she thought she'd stepped into Las Vegas.

"Wow." Ellie gulped, her eyes wide. "This place gives new meaning to excessive."

He laughed and got out of the truck.

"Albert, can you give me a hand?" Wyatt's voice held a certain reserve when he spoke to the boy, but Ellie thought he was getting used to thinking of Albert as someone other than the enemy.

"Can I go, too?" Gracie said as she reached for her seat belt.

"Not this time." Wyatt winked at her. "It's a surprise."

Frustrated but also curious, Gracie kept watch until she saw the two males returning. "They didn't get anything," she said, disappointed.

"Don't judge by what you see," Albert told her. "Christmas is all about believing. Gran used to say nobody would believe God would send His son as a baby in a manger where animals were, but that's exactly what He did."

A little thrill wiggled inside Ellie when Wyatt smiled at her, delighted when he suggested prolonging the fun by treating them all to ice cream.

Back at his ranch Gracie squealed with excitement when she saw a conical shape sitting in a massive pot on the front step.

"It's a Christmas tree!"

"See, Gracie? You have to believe," Albert told her. "Wyatt had it delivered while we had ice cream." His chest puffed out a little. "I helped pick it out."

"Good job." Ellie applauded. "It's gorgeous and much better than a fake tree."

"Or cutting one down." Wyatt unlocked the

door and waited for everyone to enter before he carried in the tree. "It's an Aleppo pine tree. I'll plant it when Christmas is over. In ten years I'll have a nice grove of trees. If it survives," he muttered as Cade yanked on a bough.

They immediately began to decorate it. Within minutes Ellie was doubled over in laughter.

"It's not funny," Wyatt growled as he lifted off the strand of lights Gracie had tossed on, and rearranged them more symmetrically.

"It's hilarious." She chuckled even harder watching his face as the kids hung ornaments willy-nilly. Like a robot on overdrive Wyatt unhooked and rehooked them, trying to keep up. "Give up. It's a Christmas tree, Wyatt. Not a work of art."

Ellie felt awful for saying that when his face got a stricken look, and he left to sit rigidly on the sofa.

"I'm sorry," she apologized. "It's your tree and your home. You should decorate it the way you want."

"Do you know what I was doing?" he whispered, his voice ragged. "I was doing exactly what my father did to me. In all my years of living with him I never managed to hang even one Christmas decoration the way he wanted. I was trying to decorate the tree as he wanted, and he's not even here to see."

Ellie couldn't stand seeing his pain, so she leaned over and threaded her fingers in his. "So you'll change. Right?"

"Absolutely." He squeezed her fingers, then covered their clasped hands with his other one. "Thank you, Ellie."

"No." She shook her head as she pulled her hand free, desperate to move away before she did something rash—like kiss him again. "Thank *you* for making this such a fun time for them." She nodded toward the kids.

"For me, too," was all Wyatt said, but when she relaxed against the sofa, Wyatt's arm somehow crept behind her head and rested above her shoulders. And she liked it.

"Christmas is coming together, isn't it?" she said later after he'd put Cade to bed and Albert was sitting in a corner reading the Christmas story to Gracie. "What do you hope for Christmas, Wyatt?"

"Finding out about my mother would be the perfect gift." He grinned. "I might get it, too."

"Oh?"

"I just got a text. I'm getting a report about her tomorrow." When Wyatt turned his head, Ellie caught her breath at the hopeful yet wary look she saw there. "Can you pray about it?" he asked.

"Absolutely." For the second time that night she reached out and took his hand. And this time she hung on, tamping down her own feelings to offer support and encouragement to him. But inside she was whispering a totally different prayer than the one he requested.

This man has a place in my heart, God, and I know that's not Your will for me. So what am I supposed to do about it?

"Esau doesn't understand why he's wearing this strange harness, Gracie." Wyatt gazed down at her as she regarded the fidgeting pony. "That's why we need you to help him get used to it. Okay?"

"Yeah." Lately the little girl had seemed down, despite the fast approach of Christmas. Wyatt was pretty sure it had to do with him and his refusal to be the daddy she longed for, but he wasn't sure how to fix it other than the obvious solution, and he wasn't going to do that even though he'd grown very fond of Gracie.

"You're sad today." It felt like her tiny fist squeezed his heart when she bowed her head. "Can you tell me why?"

After a very long silence, Gracie lifted her head, her eyes locking with his. "Why doesn't God answer prayers?"

Nothing like an easy question.

"What makes you think He doesn't?"

She gave him a look of disdain.

"You mean about me being your daddy?"

She nodded glumly.

Wyatt frowned. "But that's not the only thing bothering you, is it?"

She shook her head.

"I'm no good at guessing. You have to tell me what's wrong, Gracie."

"It's not just my prayers." Her bottom lip trembled. "It's lots of people's."

"Like?" Wyatt had no clue how to deal with this, but some inner warning compelled him to keep her talking. "Who else doesn't get their prayers answered?"

"You."

Wyatt blinked in surprise. "Me?"

"Uh-huh." Gracie looped the horse's reins around the saddle's pommel. "You been prayin' to find your mommy, but God doesn't answer."

Her words and the sympathy in her gaze touched his heart. What a dear, sweet child she was. Any father would be proud to call Gracie his.

"My mom has been gone a long time. Maybe God needs some time to find her," he explained. The day was almost over, and the investigator still hadn't called.

"God doesn't need time," Gracie scoffed. "He can do what He wants when He wants to."

"Then maybe I need time." Torn by anticipation that perhaps today he'd finally learn the truth about his mother and yet hesitant to have those years-long questions answered, Wyatt had a hunch Gracie would understand his issues. "Do you want to know a secret?"

Gracie's eyes widened as she slowly nodded.

"I'm a little bit scared to meet my mother." It felt good to admit that.

"Why?" Gracie's forehead pleated in a frown. "'Cause maybe she won't like you?"

"Something like that," he admitted, giving voice to what had hidden inside him for years. "Maybe that's why she went away, because she didn't like me."

"Nah. You're nice, so I don't think that's why." Gracie's staunch support made him chuckle. "'Sides, mommies always like their kids."

Wyatt didn't have the heart to tell her it wasn't always true, but he didn't have to because Gracie found her own answer.

"Maybe not." She frowned again. "Albert's mommy left him, and he's been prayin' a long time for her to come back." She heaved a giant sigh. "So why doesn't God answer our prayers?"

"There might be lots of reasons, and I doubt we'll ever know all of them." That answer was weak as water. Wyatt wanted desperately to reassure this sweet child so he hurried on. "I think the important thing is to keep talking to God and trusting that He'll do His best for us."

"I guess." Gracie's face looked only a little less glum.

"So can you try riding Esau again now?" he asked, feeling like he'd failed her. "Hold the reins as I showed you and lean back, just the way you think Esther would."

"But I don't even know her," Gracie complained.

"You'll meet her soon," he said, hoping he could keep his word.

"How's it going?" Ellie called from her stance by the fence rail. She gave Gracie an encouraging smile. "Looks good, sweetie."

"Can you stay here with her for a minute?" he asked her because he'd just figured out the problem. "I need to get Tanner, so he can see what I mean about an adjustment. I'll be back in a minute."

It took a little longer than that. By the time Wyatt returned, Albert had appeared and was trying to persuade Gracie to put her feet in the stirrups.

"It makes the horse feel better," he said as if he were a riding pro.

"But it makes *my* legs hurt," Gracie complained. "They don't fit."

"Exactly." Wyatt turned to Tanner. "See what I was saying?"

They mulled it over for a few moments, then came up with a solution.

"Am I done now?" Gracie finally asked. "'Cause I gotta go to the practice."

"Choir rehearsal for their concert," Ellie explained when Wyatt sent her a questioning look. "After that we're going caroling at a seniors' home. Want to come?"

"That's why I stayed after the class today," Albert explained. "I'm going, too."

"I'll go with you." Wyatt made the snap decision because there was still nothing from the investigator, and it was driving him nuts.

Ellie gave him a big smile. "Glad to have you." Her dazzling grin did funny things to Wyatt's midsection.

"I'll have to bring Cade—"

"I can look after him," Albert volunteered. His face got a little red when all eyes focused on him. "I like little kids," he said defensively. "And Cade's cute."

"Thanks, Albert." Wyatt felt a kindling of a connection with the boy. Now that he knew Albert better, he realized he wouldn't have been part of the joyriding bunch that killed Taryn. Something inside him yearned to befriend him, but he hesitated. What if he failed Albert?

"'S'cuse me,'" Gracie said in a loud voice, exasperation all over her face. "Can I get down *now*?"

"Yes." Wyatt hid his grin as he lifted her off Esau's back. "You've been a great help. Thank you, Gracie."

"Welcome." She smiled at him as if they shared a secret. And maybe they did.

Wyatt was about to leave with the horse when she tugged on his pant leg and motioned him to bend down. When he did Gracie stood on tiptoe, cupped her hand around his ear and whispered.

"Don't be scared no more. If I pray about finding your mom really hard, maybe God'll answer that prayer."

She was such a sweetheart. A lump lodged in Wyatt's throat, making it impossible for him to speak. So he simply nodded then, without thought, hugged her tightly. If only—

"I gotta go now," she whispered this time much louder, giving a slight wiggle to get free.

"So we'll meet you at the church?" Ellie studied the two of them with a confused look.

"After I get Cade, you mean? Okay." Wyatt had a hunch he was getting entirely too dependent on the lovely Ellie for company, but how could he not?

Ellie was the very spirit of Christmas, baking goodies, insisting he get a tree and helping decorate his house. He felt a rush of warmth inside him whenever he thought about the bighearted nurse who spread cheer wherever she went.

His life would be so boring without Ellie.

But he couldn't care for her as more than a friend, and even that was risky because he always ended up failing people.

Wyatt snapped himself out of that vein of thought, then noticed Albert standing just beyond the circle of their group, as if he felt left out. Wyatt knew exactly how that felt. He made a sudden decision.

"Want to come with me, Albert?"

A surprised look flickered across the boy's face before he gave a nod. "Sure."

"I'll meet you at my truck in five minutes, after I unsaddle Esau." Wyatt walked the horse toward the tack room. Lefty met him halfway and insisted he'd take care of Esau. Wyatt was almost to his truck when his phone rang.

The private investigator. Finally he'd know the truth about his mother.

"Albert, did something happen with Wyatt?" Ellie murmured as they waited for the vet to unbuckle his son from his car seat and join the choir that was to sing at the seniors' home. Earlier she'd met Wyatt at the church as they'd planned then spent the entire choir rehearsal trying to figure out what was wrong with him. "He seems...sad."

"He got a phone call before we left Wranglers Ranch," Albert said. "I think it was something about his mom."

Ellie sucked in her breath on a silent prayer that the news hadn't been bad. Wyatt so needed answers. Maybe if he—

"Sorry to hold you up for the caroling." He led Cade by the hand as he approached.

"The seniors are going to love him." Ellie helped the choir leaders shepherd the children inside to a large room.

Knowing their part, the kids assembled immediately, smiled at the seniors and, when given a chord, burst into a series of songs they were going to sing at their Christmas concert in a few days. She had to laugh when Wyatt set Cade down and the boy immediately headed for the Christmas tree with its glittering decorations. Wyatt, busy texting on his phone, didn't seem to notice Cade's disappearance, so Ellie scooped the child into her arms and took him to the back of the room where she gave him a toy truck to play with.

"Sorry." Wyatt's face was pale when he caught up. "I should have been paying more attention."

"No problem." Ellie couldn't ignore the trouble brewing in Wyatt's eyes as he gazed at his phone. "What's wrong?"

"Nothing." He quickly shoved the phone in his pocket.

"Haven't we gotten past the social niceties yet?" she said in a very quiet voice. "Please, tell me what's wrong."

"The investigator found my mother." He said the words without emotion.

"Isn't that good news?" But she could see from his haggard look that it wasn't. Fear snuck in and grabbed Ellie by the throat. "Wyatt?"

"My mother is in a care home," he said. "A care home for mentally unstable people. She's been there for nearly twenty-eight years, Ellie."

Oh, Lord. Help him. Please, help him. Heal his hurting heart.

When the silence between them stretched too long and she couldn't stand it anymore, she said, "It doesn't change who you are, Wyatt."

"Doesn't it?" His dark eyes seemed frozen.

"Of course not. She has an illness, and she's in a place where they can treat it. That's something to be thankful for." Ellie felt as if her words were bouncing off him but she didn't know what else to say to break his stony demeanor.

"Why didn't my father tell me?" The words seemed pulled out of him. "Why let me go on wondering, thinking she'd abandoned me?" His tortured words begged her for an answer. "If the dates are right I was barely two when she left. Maybe he couldn't have told me then, but why not later on when I asked about her?"

"He didn't tell you anything?" Her heart ached for him. If only she could ease this burden for the man she loved.

"When I was eighteen, just before I left for college, I asked him if he knew where my mother was or if she was dead." Wyatt lifted Cade and cradled him in his arms so the weary boy could rest his head on his daddy's shoulder. "He said she was never coming back, and that was the end of it. We never spoke of it again."

"I'm sorry." She placed her hand on his arm, wishing she could bear some of his pain. "Do you know where the care home is?"

"Right here in Tucson." His lips pressed in a tight line of anger. "Eventide Rest Home." He made a face. "Would you believe I made a call there recently to treat an injured cat? I was in the same place as my mother, and I never even knew it."

Anger and pain oozed through the words. But Ellie needed to help this man she loved see past the pain to the opportunity.

"You have to go see her," she said firmly. "Talk to her, find out what you can. Get your questions answered." As the choir neared the end of their final song, she asked, "Did your investigator say you could do that?"

"He didn't say." Wyatt frowned. "You think I should go there?"

"Don't you want to?" She couldn't believe he didn't.

"Yes, but—" He swallowed hard. "What if she isn't able to tell me anything?"

"Then you'll know." The children were bowing to their audience's applause. They only had seconds before they'd be interrupted. "Tomorrow, Wyatt. You go after work and get the answers you want. All right?"

Wyatt didn't answer until they were outside in the parking lot, the kids buckled in.

"I'd like to go tomorrow," he said for her ears alone. "And I'd be very grateful if you would come with me, Ellie, because I don't think I can do this alone."

"I'll go with you," she assured him. "And so will God. He's known the truth all along. And now you'll learn it, too."

Cars pulled out of the parking lot as the rest of the choir left. Wyatt stared at her for so long that eventually they were the only ones left in the lot. Finally, he spoke.

"I've never known anyone quite like you, Ellie." His voice was low, deep. "You go way above and beyond, as if you can never give quite enough. You're like the song, making spirits bright wherever you go." He leaned forward and brushed his lips against hers and then suddenly, he deepened the kiss, showing her without words that he cared about her.

At least that's what she thought he was showing her.

Ellie kissed him back because she couldn't help herself. Wyatt was the man of her dreams. He held her heart in his hands, though he didn't know it.

You're not free to love him, her brain whispered. *You gave your life, your wants, your dreams and your future to God. And He's given you Gracie to care for. That has to be enough.*

The thought sobered her like a snowball in the face. Ellie drew back, breaking the kiss.

"Get some rest, Wyatt," she whispered. "Tomorrow's going to be a big day. Good night."

"Good night," he called just before she closed her car door.

"You were kissing my da—you were kissing *him*," Gracie accused. "Me 'n Albert saw you."

"Be quiet now, Gracie," Albert admonished softly. Then he looked at Ellie. "I could take the bus home."

"Be quiet, Albert," she said, unable to stem the spill of tears down her cheeks.

The ride to his home was utterly silent. When

they pulled up to the curb, a large man in a tattered T-shirt came barreling down the walk, yanked open the car door and dragged out a cringing Albert.

"You're late," he said in a furious voice. "I told you to be here at eight."

"I'm sorry, sir," Ellie apologized. "It's my fault we're late. I—" She caught her breath when the man turned on her, his eyes blazing hate.

"Leave, lady," he ordered with menace. "And don't come back." Then he looked at Albert. "Get into the house."

Ellie clearly saw fear in Albert's eyes. How she wished Wyatt was here. But just because he wasn't didn't mean she'd leave without trying to make Albert's life easier.

"Excuse me?" She cringed when the man wheeled around with a sneer. "You don't have to be so mean," she said in her firmest nurse voice. "He's just a boy."

"I'm the only thing standing between him and reform school, so I'll talk to him any way I please. Butt out, lady." After another sneering glare the man stomped toward the house.

Ellie drove home with a terrible feeling that Albert was going to pay for her interference.

"Is that mean man going to hit Albert again?" Gracie asked in a voice brimming with fear.

Again?

"Did he hit Albert before?" Ellie asked as nonchalantly as she could.

"Lots of times, Albert said. Can't you stop it, Mommy?"

"I'm going to try," she promised grimly.

Later, once Gracie was in bed, she phoned Wyatt and asked for the number of his investigator.

"Why?"

Ellie admitted what had happened.

"I'm going to have him investigate Albert's uncle. Maybe then the boy won't have to live there."

"Where *will* he live?" Wyatt asked.

"I don't know. Somewhere where he's not terrified, I hope," she said staunchly.

"That's my Ellie. Spreading love and happiness wherever she can."

My Ellie? How she wanted to be!

Wyatt's chuckle didn't sound like he was making fun of her. It sounded tender. Maybe even affectionate.

"Isn't that what a Christian is supposed to do?" she finally asked, then quickly added, "See you tomorrow, Wyatt," before she hung up.

Ellie turned on the Christmas tree, switched on the electric fireplace and stared into the flickering light.

"I'm scared, God. I've let myself fall in love with Wyatt. Please, help me."

Ellie's Christmas list dangled on the fridge, but for once she didn't try to check off anything. For this one moment she sat silent, waiting for God to show her how to get over a very handsome vet to whom she'd given her heart.

Chapter Twelve

"Albert's scared stiff of his uncle. I can't just let that go." Ellie's passionate voice made him proud of having her for a friend.

"I wish you'd waited till I could be there." Wyatt grimaced as he drove toward the place where his mother lived. "But I'm glad you talked to the social worker and that she's laying down the law to his uncle." Because he guessed Ellie was already stretched thin in the finance department, Wyatt had instructed the investigator she'd hired to send him the bill.

"Why are you so quiet?" she asked moments later.

"I saw something this morning at Wranglers Ranch that really got to me." With school closed for Christmas break, the ranch was full of youngsters. But one in particular had drawn his attention today.

"I saw Albert," he said.

"So did I." Something about the way she said it made Wyatt glance at her. Her lips were pursed, and she was frowning. "He was clutching his side, but when I asked him about it, he said he'd bumped into something."

"Like maybe his uncle?" Wyatt inwardly fumed. "I hope that social worker acts fast. He needs to be out of there if there's even a suspicion of abuse."

"I have way more than a suspicion." Ellie grimaced. "Anyway, you were saying?"

"Albert was talking to a kid in the corner of the tack room. Gracie was hiding around the corner outside. She had dirt on her face, and I think she'd been crying." Wyatt held the picture in his mind. "They were all quick to make an excuse and leave when they saw me, but—Ellie, I think Albert was defending Gracie."

"Defending her?" Ellie frowned at him. "From what?"

"Whom," Wyatt corrected. He wished now that he'd talked to Albert first before he worried Ellie. But it was too late for regrets. "I only overheard a little of what Albert said."

She poked his side when he didn't immediately speak. "What did you hear, Wyatt?"

"I thought I heard him say, 'We don't bully little kids at Wranglers Ranch.'" When Ellie didn't respond, he glanced at her.

"Gracie's had mud on her shirt a couple of times, and once she had a tear on her jeans, but she never said anybody was bullying her." Ellie sounded shocked.

"Maybe she didn't know that's what it was. But Albert did." He studied his hands on the wheel, trying to sort through his feelings. "Does he know because he's suffered the same thing?"

"I don't know." Ellie sighed as she stretched out her legs. "It's so hard being a single parent. You have to be constantly aware of every detail in your kid's life and if you miss one tiny thing—" She couldn't finish.

"We'll talk to them both when we get back," Wyatt promised. "We'll sort it out. Don't worry. I just thought you should know." He took the exit ramp toward Eventide Rest Home, trying to ignore the stir of uneasiness in his stomach.

He was going to see his mother, a woman he'd stopped hoping was alive.

He parked in the visitors' lot, then looked around. It was a typical one-level care facility spread out over an area with lovely winding paths and raised beds burgeoning with flowering pansies in a host of different colors. Brown wicker deer wearing big red bow ties stood here and there throughout the landscape, tiny lights covering them. At night it would look like they'd come to feed.

"I guess we should go in." He pulled his keys from the ignition. "My appointment with the administrator, Graham Parker, is in five minutes."

"Are you ready for this?" Ellie waited while he thought about it, then finally nodded.

Before they got out, she reached for his hand. Her warm capable fingers closed around his and gently squeezed, imparting comfort and solidarity, as if she knew he was a quaking mass of jelly inside. In his mind one question grew to gigantic proportions.

What if his mother wanted nothing to do with him?

As they walked up the path to the main door Wyatt wondered if he'd ever be able to forgive his father.

They went in and were ushered in to see the administrator.

"We didn't know Mrs. Wright had a son," Mr. Parker said, studying Wyatt from his seat behind a massive desk.

"I didn't know I had a mother," Wyatt shot back, frustrated by the man's need to chat. "May we please see her now? You understand if I'm impatient after all these years."

"Of course. But I must caution you. Your mother has days when things are crystal clear in her mind. Then she has times when she's terribly confused." The administrator narrowed his gaze. "If she becomes agitated, my staff will ask you to leave. Mrs. Wright's comfort is our primary concern."

"As it should be." Wyatt had to ask one more question. "How is her care paid for?"

"By an annuity. Her husband set it up. As I understand the terms, it will take care of everything she needs until she, er, doesn't need it anymore."

"I see." Anger burned at his father's actions. Why the secrecy?

"Are you ready?" Mr. Parker rose and walked to the door. "I'll take you."

"Maybe I should wait here, Wyatt." Ellie hung back. "This is a special moment between the two of you. You don't need me there."

"Yes, I do." He reached for her hand and clung to it. "I need you with me, Ellie." The words came from his heart, without forethought. But they were the truth.

He *did* need her. Ellie was the glue that held his days together. It was she who had brought back his joy in Christmas, her and Gracie. Maybe he was being selfish, but at the moment Wyatt couldn't imagine taking this next step without Ellie at his side.

As they walked down the hall, her hand in

his was about the only thing that kept him from turning tail and getting out of there.

Mr. Parker stopped. "Here we are." After giving a quick rap on the door, he pushed it open and stepped inside. "Hello, Ruth. You have visitors today. This is Wyatt and Ellie."

Wyatt stood gazing at the woman seated in a soft blue upholstered rocker. Her hair was long and tied to the top of her head, sandy brown like his. Her eyes shone a dark brown—also like his—as she peered up at them through small gold-framed glasses. She was delicate-looking, as if one of Tucson's windstorms might pick her up and toss her away.

"Hello. Have you come to help me decorate the Christmas tree? It will soon be Christmas, you know." Her voice was soft and musical. She clasped her hands together and smiled. "I do so love Christmas, though some call my decorations geegaws."

Ellie's glance shifted from him to the paper chains covering the table in front of his mother. Wyatt knew she was recalling the time he'd used the same word when she'd been decorating his house. But he couldn't take his eyes off his mother.

"Please, do sit down." She glanced around. "I think the teapot's here somewhere."

"No tea for me, thank you, Ruth." Ellie sat

across from his mother on the small footstool. "These are very lovely," she said fingering the chains. "You've done so many."

"I have a large tree to decorate." She frowned suddenly and peered at him. "Your name is Wyatt?" He nodded. "Oh, how wonderful." She smiled and leaned toward him to whisper, "I have a son named Wyatt, you know. He's such a sweet boy."

Wyatt moved behind Ellie and let his hands rest on her shoulders as he listened to his mother recall his birth and the first few months of his life. Ellie's hands covered his, lending him the strength to stay still and listen to his own history. But then his mother's memories grew vague, confused, and she began to ramble.

"I couldn't stay because I was ill," she whispered, peeking over one shoulder and then the other. "Everything kept going wrong, and he blamed me."

"You mean my father, Bernard, your husband?" Wyatt asked, speaking for the first time since they'd arrived.

"You mustn't say his name. That's the rule." She began rocking back and forth, repeating, "That's the rule."

"Ruth—uh—" Was he supposed to call her that? Wyatt didn't know, but there were so many things he wanted to ask her, so many blanks to fill in. He stepped forward, placed his hand on top of hers. "Can you tell me—"

"No. Can't tell." She reared away from him, crossed her arms in front of her and resumed rocking back and forth.

"I'm sorry, but Ruth can't visit anymore." A pleasant-faced woman stood in the open doorway. "You'll have to leave now."

"But I need to know—" Wyatt froze as his mother screamed.

"Can't tell. Can't ever tell. No. No," she shrieked.

"We have to make decorations, Ruth." Ellie quickly and carefully laid a paper chain in her lap, her tone calming. "Here's yours. What a lovely thing it is. See how it dances in the light. How shall we hang it on the tree? I know. We'll use ribbons. Bright red ribbons. And maybe we can add some silver bells."

As Wyatt watched, Ruth slowly relaxed, put her hands down and was soon humming "Silent Night" along with Ellie as they rolled and taped foil bits.

"She's a great one, your wife," the attendant murmured to Wyatt. "Knows exactly what our Ruth needs to calm her."

Wyatt ignored the "wife" comment, though it caused a hundred pictures to flash through his mind. Ellie mothering Cade, coaxing his Christmas spirit by baking succulent treats, playing checkers with Albert and Gracie, laughing and smiling and making the world a better place for all of them.

"Don't worry, son." The attendant patted him on the back. "Next time you visit Ruth will have a better day. No good talking to her anymore now, though."

"But I need to ask—" He wasn't sure what. He only knew he couldn't leave yet. Not with all his questions unanswered.

"Ruth can't tell you any more today, Wyatt. She's worn herself out." Ellie moved beside him, whispering as they watched his mother's frail chest rise and fall. "She needs to sleep."

"Come back another time," the attendant said as she ushered them through the doorway. "Tomorrow." Then she closed the door behind them.

Speechless, Wyatt walked beside Ellie out of the building and over to his truck. Then he paused, tilted his face up and let the sun chase away the chill he'd felt the moment Ruth had become hysterical.

"Are you okay?" Ellie asked him.

"I don't know what I am, but I don't think okay applies." He checked his watch. "Do you have time for coffee?"

"I have all the time you need, Wyatt."

Her voice, the gentleness of her response, the tender way she slid his keys from his fingers and ushered him in to his own truck and then drove them to a café reminded Wyatt of the loving care a mother would give her child. It caused a feeling he'd craved but never known in his entire life, a feeling of acceptance, of understanding.

"Tell me what you're thinking," she said when they were seated in a booth and cradling steaming mugs of coffee.

"I don't know." He tried to list the emotions he recognized. "Shock, surprise, pain, yearning, love. Hate," he added bitterly.

"Hate for your father." When he nodded, she brushed her knuckles against his cheek. "You don't know why he did this, Wyatt. You don't know the details or what drove his decision to put her there."

"No, I don't. Because he never told me." He leaned into her touch, loving the way being with Ellie brought his world back on its axis. "Why? That's what I can't get past. Why did he do it, and why did he never tell me about her?"

"Can you face never knowing?" Her eyes caressed him as she spoke. "Can you love your mother in spite of what he did? Because I think that's the only choice you have. Love her and squeeze every moment of joy and happiness you can from the relationship."

"To make up for the past, you mean?" He loved the way her lips tipped up at the corner, the way her curls bounced when she shook her head and how her eyes chided him for looking for the easy way out.

"You can't make up for the past, Wyatt. It's long gone. All you have, all any of us have, is today, this moment." Her hand dropped from his face, leaving a chill. How he craved her touch. "That's why it's so important that we make today the very best we can."

"How am I supposed to do that, Ellie? Clearly she's incapable of giving me the answers I need." He half smiled, remembering. "Gracie had a good question the other day. She asked me why God didn't answer her prayer for a daddy. I gave her platitudes." He grimaced. "Now *I'm* asking why He didn't answer my prayers for my mom."

He expected comfort, sympathy, understanding. As usual Ellie surprised him.

"Get over it, Wyatt."

He blinked, stunned by her tough response.

"What difference would knowing make at this point?" Her gaze probed his as her voice softened. "We all want answers. Why didn't God heal my sister so she could raise her baby? But what difference does asking make? It only paralyzes us."

"So how did you handle your questions?" he demanded, slightly irritated.

"The same as you. I had tantrums for a while,

demanded God explain Himself to me." She made a face. "Thing was, there was this bawling baby who needed a mom, and I was the one available, so finally I got down to the business of being her mom."

"It's not the same."

"Isn't it?" She leaned forward, her voice now oozing kindness. "You have your mother, a woman you claim to have wanted to know for years. Forget about your father, and seize this opportunity to get to know Ruth. God has given you your mom, Wyatt. What are you going to do with *that* answer?"

"You're really something, Ellie Grant," he said in amazement.

"Thank you. I think." She frowned as her phone pealed. "It's Tanner." She answered, then listened, cheeks paling a pasty white. "We'll check it out," she promised before she hung up.

"What's wrong?" Wyatt watched her gather her belongings and knew this was serious.

"Albert didn't show for this evening's dinner that Tanner's holding for his group. Apparently his uncle picked him up earlier and insisted he go home. Albert never came back, and nobody at his house is answering the phone." Fear whitened her face. "That dinner was a big deal to Albert. I can't believe he'd be a no-show without a word to anyone. Something's wrong, and I need to go to his place to find out what."

"Okay." Wyatt rose, tossed some money on the table and held out his hand. "Let's go. And this time, I'm driving."

"You have to," she murmured as they left the café. "I'm a mess of nerves. Why would his uncle prevent him from coming?"

Wyatt flung his arm around Ellie's shoulders and hugged her against his side as they walked to the truck. It felt wonderful to have a chance to comfort her this time. As they walked, Wyatt sent a prayer heavenward for Albert's safety.

"A very smart nurse told me to stop asking why and act instead. That's what we have to do now, Ellie. We need to be bold and seize this opportunity to help Albert. We need to trust God to show us what to do."

"Agreed." Ellie climbed in, then slid across the seat so she was next to him. "Thank you for caring about him, Wyatt," she murmured.

They needed to leave, but Wyatt took a few seconds to enjoy her lovely face before he dipped his head and kissed her.

"We can do this, Ellie. You and I and God."

"Sounds like a great combination."

Chapter Thirteen

"Looking a little haggard there, Wyatt." Tanner bumped his veterinarian in the arm with a smirk. "Foster parenthood wearing you down already?"

"No, Albert's great. It's potty training Cade that's killing me." Wyatt chuckled. "You'll find out soon enough." He winked at Ellie. "Won't he?"

She nodded, though she thought Wyatt looked great. In fact, she let her eyes feast on him as the men talked.

"Don't know how you persuaded the social worker to let Albert come to your place," Tanner was saying, more serious now. "But I'm sure glad you did. I'm gathering from his broken arm and what Sophie's managed to pry out of him these last two days, he had it pretty rough at the uncle's."

"It wasn't a matter of persuading the social

worker," Ellie explained. "Foster spaces are pretty full this time of year. Since Wyatt has previously fostered, he was a perfect candidate. And Albert loves it at his ranch."

"How long will he stay?" Tanner asked.

"Hopefully, until after Christmas."

"He can't leave now," Ellie blurted. "He belongs with people who care about him."

"I had this thought—maybe it's a stupid one but uh—anyway I thought maybe I should petition the court to give me custody. I mean he's a good kid and…" Relieved to have finally blurted out his thoughts, Wyatt smiled at her surprise. "Albert's got a lot of potential."

"That's a great idea!" Ellie couldn't believe he was willing to do that. A phone call took Tanner away, but she remained seated on the patio across from Wyatt, eager to hear more about his plans to get involved in Albert's life.

"The kid's had some bad breaks. I think he could really make something of himself, and I'd like to help him. Have you seen how great he is with the horses?" he asked, his face animated. "He's sure got the touch."

"Oh, no." Ellie clapped a hand over her mouth in pretended horror. "Are you going to try to make him over as your father tried with you?" she teased.

"I'm never going to try to mold either Cade or Albert into something they don't want to be. They have to make their own choices." He winked. "I learned that much from my father."

"I'm glad." She slid her hand across the bench and slipped it in to his. "And I think it's wonderful that you're helping Albert. God will bless you." Why wasn't holding his hand enough for her? Why did she crave more from Wyatt than a smile or a shared laugh? Why couldn't she stop wanting his love?

"Your Christmas party's still on for tonight, right?" He waited for her nod. "Can I help?"

"Thanks, but I'll manage." But how she loved him for offering.

"That's not the point. I'm your friend, and I'd like to help."

Friend? Is that all?

"Thank you." She shrugged. "It's just a cookout for a few friends, nothing special."

"If it's done by Ellie Grant, it will be special." Wyatt's dark eyes held hers for a space of time that seemed to stretch forever. "Because you're special, Ellie. Especially to me." Then Wyatt leaned forward and kissed her.

It wasn't a dreamy kind of kiss. It was quick and fast, the briefest of caresses. But it still made her toes tingle and her heart race long after Wyatt had left.

"Are you dreaming of getting *who* you want for Christmas?" Sophie came outside and sank onto the bench across from Ellie.

"You mean 'what,'" Ellie corrected.

"No, I don't." Sophie snickered.

"You finished your catering job early," Ellie said, hoping to divert her attention.

"No digressing. Your love for Wyatt is as transparent as Gracie's so-called 'secret' giant cookie gift that I've been helping her make for Cade. Oh, don't do that," she pleaded when Ellie began to cry.

"I think of Wyatt all the time," Ellie sobbed, unable to stifle it any longer. "He's such a wonderful man. He's great with Gracie, and he's even going to apply for Albert's guardianship. What's not to love?" she wailed.

"Then, what's the problem?" Sophie asked. "Are you afraid he won't reciprocate if you tell him how you feel?"

"I can't tell him how I feel! You know I can't."

"I do?" Sophie frowned and shook her head. "No, Ellie, I don't know why you can't tell him your feelings. Wyatt is a godly man who clearly cares about you. He wouldn't be kissing you so often if he didn't."

"He just sees me as a friend," she clarified

with a sniff. "But it's not his feelings I'm talking about. It's mine. I can't love him. Or anyone," she added.

"I guess this pregnancy has really impaired my brain because I don't understand anything you're saying. Why can't you love Wyatt?"

Ellie heaved a sigh. "You told me I couldn't love him, remember?"

"Me? I don't think I said that." Sophie studied her. "Refresh my memory."

"After I became a Christian, and Eddie and I broke up, you said I shouldn't be sad about it, that God was protecting me, so I could be the kind of mother Gracie needs." Ellie could tell Sophie didn't yet understand. "You said that the breakup was part of God's plan for my life, to enable me to focus on Gracie. So that's why I can't love Wyatt, because God wants me to focus on raising my daughter."

"But not exclusively!" Sophie looked shocked. "I didn't mean you couldn't ever love anyone again." She touched Ellie's cheek, her face full of compassion. "Sweetie, you can't interpret one romantic mistake as God's refusal to give you a family. I'm so sorry if I led you to think that."

"You mean it's okay with God if I love Wyatt?" Ellie studied her friend with a heart full of hope.

"Well, I think you should ask Him about it,

but I don't see why not." Sophie smiled a fleeting smile. "God is love, and I believe He wants us to love fully and from the heart. But a word of warning here. You need to remember that Wyatt has issues with the past."

"But—"

"Yes, I know you said he's coming to grips with some of them," Sophie agreed, "But I don't think he's resolved all of them. Do you?"

"No. So, what do I do? Try to maintain a friendship? Tell him how I feel and hope he feels the same? Wait?" Ellie was desperate for an answer.

"I don't have all the answers, honey. My best advice would be to keep praying for God's help. Ask Him to show you what to do with these feelings you have for Wyatt. Take your time, be sure you know where He's leading you, and then wait for Him to work it out."

"You're the best friend, and just like my sister, Karen, you always have great advice." Ellie dashed around the table to hug Sophie. "Thank you so much. And now I have to run. You're coming later, right?"

"Tanner and the kids and I wouldn't miss your party for the world, sister." Sophie hugged her back, then waved as Ellie raced to find Gracie.

All the way home her daughter sang Christmas carols while Ellie silently sang, *I love Wyatt Wright* to the same tunes.

Surely God would work it out. After all, Wyatt had kissed her in broad daylight.

Again.

Wyatt stood in the festively decorated backyard amid a score of laughing people, but he only had eyes for the hostess.

Ellie smiled when she saw him, then headed his way, threading her way through kids and adults with a word and a grin for each.

"Hi." She greeted him, then hunkered down to tickle Cade. "Hey, pumpkin."

Gracie raced over to ask if she and Beth could play with him.

"Sure," Wyatt agreed. "Just be careful he doesn't eat anything he shouldn't. Like brussels sprouts," he added when the kids had left.

Ellie burst out laughing. "That seems like a long time ago, doesn't it?"

"Eons," he agreed, unable to look away from her laughing face. He remembered he'd been a shell back then, only half-alive, unable to forgive, oblivious to the joy to be found in the world.

Ellie had changed him.

"You look deep in thought." She handed him a green-and-red punch-filled paper cup.

"I was thinking about what I was like before you and Gracie turned my world upside down." He smiled as wariness filled those lovely gray eyes. "I was a sad case back then."

"How are you doing now, Wyatt?"

"I'm good," he said, surprising himself with how true it was. "Ellie, I—" He was cut off when someone called her name. "Go ahead and circulate, Ellie. We can talk later."

"Promise?" She gazed at him in a way that made him gulp. All he could do was nod. "Okay. See you in a bit."

Wyatt spent a few moments speaking to Tanner and some other folks from church he knew, but his attention never moved far from Ellie. There was so much joy in her, so much pure delight in things he'd always found ordinary. And she never missed a detail to make someone's world special, especially his.

Wyatt had no idea how he ended up as her partner in a trivia game, but since he knew less than nothing about the answers, of course they lost.

"Punishment is to sing a duet," Sophie, the judge, declared. "How about 'The First Noel'?"

Wyatt detested the idea of standing in front of a bunch of people making an idiot of himself, but there was no way he was going to ruin Ellie's party.

"Are you up for this?" he murmured, hoping she'd say no.

"I am if you are," she said with a grin.

"Why couldn't you be a shy, quiet woman, Ellie Grant?" he groaned as she led him to the center of the group.

"Now, what's the fun in that?" she asked with a mischievous wink. "Ready?"

"As I'll ever be." Wyatt had heard Ellie's lovely voice in church so it was no hardship to sing with her. But it wasn't her voice that touched him, it was the words. When they sang the chorus, those familiar lyrics sank into his heart, reminding him of the true meaning of the story they were telling, the story of love. The story of the very first Christmas. A hush fell on the group so that even the kids gathered around, sitting on the ground to listen.

Noel, Noel, born is the King of Israel.

As their voices died away into the night, Wyatt got trapped in Ellie's gaze and something he glimpsed there—something like tenderness. Or maybe compassion.

Or perhaps—

"Okay, that's enough torture for one night," Ellie joked, easing out from under his arm.

Wyatt, still caught up in the magic of those moments when it seemed the two of them were alone together, couldn't even remember placing it on her shoulders.

"You've been holding out on our choir, Wyatt," Tanner called over the applause. "Now that we've heard you sing we'll expect you to join us."

"I don't know," Wyatt said automatically. "I have Cade—" He stopped short as he encountered Ellie's gaze. Wasn't it time to stop hiding and start participating in life?

"Everyone, come and eat," Ellie called as she moved away.

Her departure felt like a physical loss to Wyatt. He stood frozen in place as once again her yard resounded with happy people enjoying what she'd prepared. Ellie's bounty. Tons of food, masses of decorations and always laughter.

He wanted to be part of her world.

Permanently?

Wyatt studied her from a darkened corner of her yard, marveling that he was even considering the question. And yet, he was tired of being alone, of trying to manage. These past weeks of sharing with Ellie and Gracie had opened his eyes to joy, and it had been so long since he'd felt that.

He'd finally come to terms with the fact that he would never be the son his father wanted, and he couldn't spend the rest of his life trying to achieve something he didn't want.

But he could strive to be the son God wanted.

He wanted Ellie.

She'd swept into his world and prodded him back to life, despite his intention to remain aloof. Now he couldn't conceive of a day without her there to cheer and encourage him. She made him think of possibilities. He cared about Ellie Grant a great deal.

Cared about? Who was he kidding?

He loved Ellie.

The knowledge terrified him as much as it thrilled him. Relationships meant promises, and Wyatt was so lousy at keeping those. But he could learn from his past, couldn't he?

What about Gracie?

That little girl wanted a daddy so badly. Involvement with Ellie meant Wyatt better be fully committed, because Gracie needed and deserved a man who'd be there for her no matter what. He didn't think that was going to be a problem. He already loved her. But she would demand his total attention. She wanted a real daddy, not a fake or a halfway man. Wyatt suddenly realized he wanted to be that little girl's longed-for father.

But the real question was Ellie. She'd told him she wasn't interested in a relationship.

She'd also kissed him and seemed to like it when he kissed her.

Now he had to make a choice: embrace life

and love with Ellie or remain on the sidelines of life. But doing the latter meant risking becoming hard and embittered like his father.

When Wyatt weighed not having Ellie and Gracie in his life permanently, there was no contest. He wanted them both. It might take a while to convince Ellie he'd make her a good husband, but that was okay. As far as Wyatt was concerned, he had all the time in the world.

"Hey, Wyatt? Can I talk to you for a minute?" Albert shuffled his feet nervously.

"Sure." Albert would make a great addition to their family. Wyatt didn't doubt Ellie would agree with that. The boy was still quiet, but at least he was losing that nervous tenseness. "What's up?"

"I was thinking… Ellie has done a lot for me and—" Albert stopped, then started again. "I—uh, I want to give her something for Christmas."

"We can go shopping tomorrow," Wyatt promised.

"I don't have any money. Anyway I want to give her something from me, something that I put effort into."

"Okay." Wyatt wondered where this was going.

"Gracie and I were exploring the other day, and I saw some woodworking stuff in one of the sheds." He stopped, then blurted, "Can you show me how to make a wooden bowl for Ellie?"

"I haven't used my tools in a really long time." Wyatt thought of how his father had hated him working with his hands, and of how much he'd loved creating from wood. "It would be nice to share my hobby with someone." He smiled at Albert. "When do you want to start?"

"Tomorrow?"

"Right after supper," Wyatt said. "I've got something to do in the afternoon."

If Wyatt was going to move ahead with his life and loving Ellie, wasn't it about time he found out everything about his mother? Then maybe he could finally put the past behind him and embrace the future.

And then he'd tell Ellie he wanted to share that future with her.

Because he loved her.

Ellie was trying to be positive, but she couldn't quite understand Wyatt's urgency.

"Why do you need to visit her today?" she asked as he drove toward his mother's home.

"I need answers. But, first, I want to introduce her to Cade. I want him to meet his grandmother. I don't want him to spend his life asking questions about her."

She heard the underlying *As I did.*

"Good idea," she said, determined to be supportive. "I hope you brought a camera."

He nodded.

"I'm not sure she'll be able to answer your questions, though, Wyatt." She hated dashing his hopes.

"I'm not going to ask her many," he said as he turned into the parking lot. He shot her a grin full of confidence. "I'm going to talk to Mr. Parker. My investigator said he's been at Eventide for fifteen years, so he must have known my father."

"What if Mr. Parker doesn't have the answers?" Ellie was worried that Wyatt had too much vested in what he thought he'd learn today. "It might not go as you want," she cautioned.

"Ellie! Is that you with no faith?" he teased. He leaned across and tapped her on the nose. "'If God be for us, who can be against us?' Remember?"

She waited until he'd come around to open her door. He held out a hand, and she took it, unable to stop herself. How she loved this man.

"I'm sure your mother will be delighted to meet Cade." She watched as he lifted his son from the car seat, wet one fingertip and smoothed the small curl on the top of Cade's head. "What a handsome pair you make."

She clung to Wyatt's hand when the receptionist told them Mr. Parker would meet with them after they visited Wyatt's mother. She held his hand when Ruth sat holding Cade on her knee. After a few minutes, she began to call Cade Wyatt.

"Wyatt was such an active boy. I had to have three sets of eyes in my head," Ruth said. "He was so busy. He walked when he was seven months, and then it was running. Running everywhere, all the time. Such a sweet boy."

The way she, too, licked her finger and smoothed Cade's curl brought tears to Ellie's eyes. Wyatt's eyes grew damp as well when the frail woman pressed a kiss against Cade's cheek. But when the little boy began to wiggle and try to get down, Wyatt's mother seemed to fade.

Ellie took Cade to a corner of the room, so Wyatt could focus on Ruth's now faint words.

"Bernard was so busy. He seldom stayed home in the evening," she whispered. "I asked him to help me, and he always said yes, but he never had time or he forgot."

Ellie saw how deeply those words hit Wyatt. He, also, had been too busy and forgetful, and he'd spent months regretting it.

"Forgiven, Wyatt," she whispered just loud enough for him to hear. "You're forgiven."

He stared at her for a moment, then nodded,

his eyes shining. A second later he clasped his hands around his mother's.

"You did very well," he told her gently. "You were a good mother."

"I tried to be." She frowned. "But then I got sick. I had to go away."

"Did Bernard send you away?" he asked carefully.

"No! He wasn't like that. It wasn't his fault." Ruth began rocking back and forth, clearly growing more agitated. "I had to leave." She gripped his hands fiercely and stared into his face. "I had to go because something bad happened. He didn't want me to go. But I *had* to leave."

Those were her last coherent words. Suddenly she began wailing, growing more distraught with Wyatt's attempts to calm her. A moment later the attendant showed up and asked them to leave.

"Ruth *had* to go," the attendant repeated just loudly enough for them to hear.

Wyatt immediately caught on. "Yes, of course she did. We understand."

"You see, Ruth, they understand. We all do. You had to leave, and that's the way it was. Come now, dear. We'll go have some tea." With an arm around her shoulder, the woman urged Ruth out of the room.

Wyatt watched his mother leave, his hands

clenching and unclenching by his side. Finally Ellie went to him.

She wrapped her arms around him and held him. "Whatever happened back then, Ruth is all right. Your mother is fine, and she has great caregivers."

"I was the same kind of man he was." Wyatt's arms slid around her waist. He pressed his forehead against hers and spoke words that seemed to be dragged from him. "I never kept my promises, either. That's what my father taught me."

"And now your heavenly Father is teaching you a different way with Cade." She glided her fingers through his hair, loving the touch of its tight curls against her fingertips, loving the opportunity to be here, in his arms, sharing this most important moment with him. "You're not the same as your father. You're Wyatt, and you're a wonderful dad to Cade."

"I love you, Ellie Grant." Wyatt's words shocked her with their quiet intensity. Then he bent his head and kissed her the way Ellie had only ever dreamed of being kissed.

She kissed him back, pouring her heart and soul into showing him, and then, lest he not have understood, she leaned back and said, "I love you, too, Wyatt. So much."

He touched his lips to her neck, a smile in his

voice as he said, "I thought you didn't want a romantic relationship, Ellie."

"I didn't. Until you came." She kissed his jaw and the corner of his mouth and the end of his nose. "What about you?"

"I was never going to risk failing another person. I was going to focus totally on Cade." He grinned at her. "Until I fell in love with you."

"When was that?" she asked, savoring the wonderful words.

"The moment I saw you, I think." Then he kissed her again, and Ellie lost all rational thought until a squeal just outside the room separated both of them. "Where's Cade?"

"Right here." Graham Parker stood in the hall, holding Cade in his arms. "He runs fast," he said with a chuckle.

"I'm sorry." Ellie took him. "I should have been watching him more closely."

"No problem." He smiled, then looked at Wyatt. "Would you like to have that talk now?"

Wyatt nodded.

Ellie threaded her fingers in his as they walked to the administrator's office. At last Wyatt was going to get the answers he'd been waiting for.

Please, be with him now, she pleaded. *Please, please, let it be okay.*

But as soon as Mr. Parker began speaking, she knew it wouldn't be.

Chapter Fourteen

Wyatt sat in stunned silence as his questions were finally answered.

"I'm sorry to have to tell you, Mr. Wright," the administrator said as he leaned forward in his chair, "but your mother suffers from schizophrenia. She has for some time."

He felt as if a vise was clenching his heart, but he sat there, quiet and still as Mr. Parker continued.

"Mrs. Wright was brought here by her husband almost twenty-eight years ago."

"Why?" Wyatt squeezed the word out past the lump in his throat.

"I wasn't in charge then, you understand," the man said, his tone troubled. "But I checked the records for you. They indicate that she was brought in by her husband, at her request, after she left her son alone in an empty house to walk through the desert. Apparently she had some sort of break with reality. Since that day Mrs. Wright has not left our care."

"Surely she was treated?"

"Oh, yes. She's received ongoing treatment," Mr. Parker assured him. He sighed. "It has not been—shall we say, totally successful."

"But when my father died—" He tried to order his thoughts, grateful when Ellie stepped in.

"Wyatt was never informed that his mother was alive or that she was here," she told the administrator. "Why was that?"

"Quite simply, and I'm sorry if this sounds hurtful, but your father didn't want you to know." He tented his fingers.

"Why?" Wyatt couldn't stop the words from exploding from him. "Why didn't he tell me? I could have visited, talked to her, helped her. Instead I've gone all these years without knowing my mother was even alive."

Fury built inside until he could no longer sit. He jumped to his feet. When Ellie rose, too, he waved her off.

"I need some time to process this. Can you watch Cade?"

"Of course." After giving him a loving look she left with Cade.

Wyatt wandered down the hall, drawn somehow back to Ruth's room. He stood outside the open door, listening to her voice, trying to make it sink into his brain that this was his mother, the woman who'd given him life, the one who should have been sharing his life.

Wyatt wasn't sure how long he remained there before it dawned on him that Ruth was speaking to someone. He peeked around the corner but saw no one else in the room. Puzzled, he stood there, listening.

"I can't, Bernard," she said in a mournful tone. "Don't you understand? I can't take care of a child, not even my own. I'm afraid that you'll leave me alone, and I'll do something wrong again. Help me, please. Don't make me stay." Her voice dropped to a whisper. "What if I hurt him?"

Hurt him—Wyatt? She'd run away to save him? Wyatt couldn't make the pieces come together.

Confused, he walked back to the administrator's office.

"May I interrupt again?" he asked.

"Of course. Whatever I can do to help you," Mr. Parker assured him.

"Can you tell me more about her disease?"

"Certainly. Schizophrenia is a long-term mental disorder of a type involving a breakdown in the relation between thought, emotion and behavior, leading to faulty perception, inappropriate actions and feelings, withdrawal from reality and personal relationships into fantasy and delusion, and a sense of mental fragmentation." The man frowned. "Of course there are treatments."

"Drugs." Wyatt grimaced.

"Antipsychotic medications," Mr. Parker corrected. "Your mother has been treated with a number of them in different combinations but with limited success. If you wish you could certainly make an appointment to speak to her doctor."

"Why don't you give me the short version?" Wyatt suggested.

"Well, according to her records, she seems to suffer side effects from most of them, so treating her is a delicate balance." He glanced at the file in front of him. "Ruth is also receiving ongoing psychotherapy."

"Which doesn't seem to be working much if she's still having these—what did you call them—breakdowns?" Wyatt exhaled and asked the question uppermost in his mind. "Is it genetic?"

"I'm not an authority—"

"Please, just tell me what you know," Wyatt pleaded.

Mr. Parker hesitated for several moments, then spoke very quietly.

"Schizophrenia has a strong hereditary component. Individuals with a first-degree relative such as a parent or sibling who has schizophrenia have a ten percent chance of developing the disorder, as opposed to the one percent chance of the general population." The administrator sighed. "I'm sorry."

Wyatt's insides froze.

"Son," Parker said softly. "Your father believed that was the main reason your mother insisted on leaving her home and you," Parker said.

Wyatt blinked back to reality. "Excuse me?"

"She wanted to protect you." Parker shrugged. "Your father made certain she would be taken care of here at Eventide."

"But he never let me see her or even know she was here." Wyatt couldn't get past that.

"He may have shared her fears that you would get hurt."

With that comment Wyatt's lonely childhood suddenly made sense. His father's strict demands were to make sure his son didn't go off on some tangent, didn't get sidetracked. He'd pushed Wyatt to become a lawyer to be grounded in facts, as he was. Mental disease would be abhorrent to socially conscious Bernard Wright.

"Of course treatment has changed a lot. Diagnosed earlier, success rates are much better. Many people who suffer with this disease are able to manage it with medication and return to work and a normal life." Mr. Parker studied him. "I don't think you—"

"Oh, you're in here." Ellie stood in the doorway. "Sorry to interrupt, but Cade's really hungry, Wyatt."

"Yes, we need to leave." He rose, thrust out a hand to the administrator. "Thank you for explaining. I'm sorry I took so much of your time."

"Not at all. I'll walk out with you." Mr. Parker plucked a wafer out of a red Christmas tin on his desk and handed it to Ellie. "This might help with your boy."

She took it and handed it to Cade who immediately stopped weeping and began eating the treat. "Thank you."

"It's a wonderful time of year to share with a child that age." Parker led the way outside, smiling as the landscape lighting clicked on. "Kids are so inspiring. For them Christmas means anything's possible."

Anything? Like not developing schizophrenia?

"May I say one thing more?" Mr. Parker asked. "Your mother's fears are probably unfounded. But at least you know the truth now, and with advance warning you can seek treatment."

Thanks for nothing.

Parker mussed Cade's hair, urged them to visit Ruth again, then wished them a Merry Christmas.

"Let's go." Wyatt walked back to the truck, replaying everything he'd learned.

The ride home was silent. Finally, he pulled up in front of Ellie's, and when he helped her out of the truck, she grabbed the front of his jacket and stood on her tiptoes to kiss him.

"You won't get schizophrenia just because your mother has it, Wyatt." Ellie's confidence came through the whispered words.

"How can you be so sure?"

"I love you, Wyatt. And I have faith that God has something special planned for you." She touched his cheek, her eyes brimming with love.

He loved that about Ellie, that steely confidence in her heavenly Father. Truth was, he loved everything about her, from the top of her ruffled curls that never seemed to tame to her pink-tipped toenails peeking out from her sandals. She was as lovely inside as out.

But he couldn't offer her security, and therein lay his problem.

Yet neither could he walk away, not from sweet, loving Ellie.

Wyatt leaned forward and rested his lips on hers, trying to tell her without words how much he cared for her. Since the day they'd met, she'd been there for him, cheering him on, encouraging him to embrace life. He wordlessly tried to tell her how much her support, her love meant to him, infusing as much into the kiss as he could.

But Cade had woken and was not to be silenced. After several moments, Wyatt eased away.

"Thank you for coming with me," he said. He reached out and lifted one wiry curl away from her amazing eyes. "Thank you for everything, Ellie."

She stepped back, a troubled look filling her face.

"You're making this sound like goodbye," she whispered.

He smiled, squeezed her hand, then climbed back into his truck and drove away, glancing in his mirror just once to see her standing where he'd left her, staring after him.

Wyatt forced his gaze back on the road. As he drove home, his mind teemed with imaginings of leaving Cade alone as his mother left him, or worse, leaving Ellie to manage two children on her own.

No, he couldn't indulge his yearning to love Ellie and be loved by her. Doing so could ruin her life. It was better for him to make preparations for Cade. Tomorrow he'd ask Tanner and Sophie if they'd be his son's godparents.

Wyatt fed Cade but had no appetite for his own meal. He tucked his son into bed, loving the way his chubby arms reached out for a hug and a kiss. How could his mother have given this up? How much love she'd had to walk away in an effort to protect him. And his father, too? Would Wyatt be able to do the same if the time came?

Wyatt returned to his living room and sat staring at the Christmas tree until Albert arrived on the church's youth group bus.

"Was it a good Christmas party?" he asked.

"The best."

"That's good." He wouldn't be able to adopt Albert now, not with the future so uncertain. But he'd wait until after Christmas to tell him that. Albert deserved a happy, peaceful Christmas.

"You seem down." Albert studied him. "I guess you don't want to work on Ellie's bowl tonight, do you?"

"No, this is a good time, if I can get my neighbor to babysit." Wyatt pushed away his dark thoughts and picked up the phone.

The older woman readily agreed and arrived less than five minutes later.

He and Albert went out to the shed where Albert chose a piece of cherry wood from the stack Wyatt had left to dry shortly after he and Taryn had bought the ranch.

"That'll make a great bowl," he said and began showing Albert how to use the tools to create his gift for Ellie.

When they'd done all they could for the night, they returned to the house. The sitter left, and Albert went to bed. But Wyatt sat long into the night alternately praying for help and trying to make sense of the incomprehensible.

What if, even now, the genesis of this awful disease was growing inside his head, threatening to cloud his mind?

There was only one thing to do. He'd have to break off his connections with Ellie. It wasn't fair to let her keep thinking there could be something between them. Even the thought of not seeing her face every day, not hearing her laugh or working with her at Wranglers tore at him.

He loved her so much.

"Only two days until Christmas, shoppers." Gracie's shrill voice parodied the advertisement on the car radio in such a lackluster tone that Ellie's heart hurt.

"You don't seem very eager for Christmas to get here, honey." She glanced in the mirror and saw Gracie's frown. "Aren't you looking forward to Melissa's Christmas party this morning, or to giving out your cookie gifts this afternoon?"

"I guess." Gracie heaved a sigh that told the truth.

"Want to tell me what's wrong?"

"It's Wyatt."

Ellie was surprised at hearing her daughter actually call the rancher by name. What happened to Daddy?

"He's not the same anymore." Gracie frowned. "Yesterday he hardly said anything when I was ridin' the horse for the girl who's coming today. He looks sad."

"I'm sorry, sweetie." Ellie did not want to talk about Wyatt, not after the way he'd been shutting her out every time she came near him. She'd tried everything, but it was like talking to a wall. Wyatt couldn't hear her. He was shut down by fear.

"He doesn't look at you like he did, neither," Gracie mumbled.

"How did he look at me before?" Ellie asked eagerly. She'd told herself she'd only imagined him saying that he loved her because she'd wanted it to be true for so long.

"Before when he looked at you, he'd smile, like he was happy inside 'bout sumthin'." Gracie exhaled heavily. "Now I think he hurts."

Join the club.

But Ellie didn't say that. She'd prayed constantly for guidance, for words that could melt the ice of fear in him and free the heart she knew was aching. She'd also struggled to find the right words to explain his absence from their world to Gracie. But she couldn't find them.

"Have fun at the party, honey," she said as she pulled up in front of Melissa's. "They'll bring you back to Wranglers Ranch when it's over because I have to be there for the Make-a-Wish kids. Okay?"

"Yeah." Gracie unsnapped her seat belt but paused before she opened the door. "Mommy?"

"Yes, sweetie?" Ellie knew this was something important because Gracie hesitated so long before she spoke.

"God isn't going to give me a daddy, is He?" Her eyes were shiny, and she dashed a fist against them as if to stop the flow of tears. "I thought if I prayed really hard and tried to do good things that He would answer my prayer, but He isn't gonna."

So that's what was behind all the cookie gifts, Ellie realized. Gracie's sad face deepened her heartache. She got out of the car, opened Gracie's door and enfolded her child in her arms.

"Nobody can know God's plans, sweetie." She inhaled the essence of this precious child. "We have to trust He'll work things out even if it's not the way we want."

"I know." Gracie kissed her cheek, sighed, then wiggled free. "I'll keep prayin', I guess."

"Yes. And, Gracie?" Ellie straightened her ponytail, then cupped her face in her hands. "I want you to remember that you do have a Father,

God, and He loves you very much." Ellie hugged her once more. "Now throw away your sad face and have a good time with Melissa. Remember, it's Christmas."

"In two days, shoppers." Gracie giggled when her mother rolled her eyes, then dashed up the walk calling, "Bye, Mommy."

Ellie drove to Wranglers with her mind made up. She had to try once more to make Wyatt see sense. However, when she found him in the tack room with Tanner, she soon realized something had changed.

"Good morning," she greeted them both. "Big day today." Then she faced Wyatt. "When you have a minute, I'd like to talk to you."

"You can talk here if you like," Tanner said. He held out a hand to Wyatt. "I'll be sorry to see you go. I've appreciated your work with us. Thanks for staying today. God bless you." He walked away, leaving them alone.

"What does Tanner mean? Where are you going?" Icy fingers clutched at her heart.

"I gave him my notice. Today's my last day."

"Why?" She touched his sleeve while inside she begged God to change his mind. "I love you, Wyatt. Doesn't that mean anything to you?"

"It means everything." He eased away, his voice ragged. "I love you, too. But I won't saddle you with a future like I may have."

"You don't know—"

"I can't risk it, Ellie, not knowing I could end up in the same place as my mother. You'd have two kids to take care of alone." He shook his head, his voice sounding tortured as he continued. "I'll finish out today at Wranglers, but then I'm gone from here. I have to—"

"What?" she demanded angrily. "Prepare for a future where you lose your mind?" It hurt to see his pain. "Where's your faith, Wyatt? Where's your trust in God, your real Father?"

"I'm sorry." He touched her lips briefly with his, then walked away.

Heartbroken, Ellie stared after him for a long time, fighting back tears. Then she went to her office to prepare for their guests. In the ensuing hours she devoted herself to the sick children that visited the ranch, doing her utmost to make their time at Wranglers a dream come true. But each time she glimpsed Wyatt, each time his turbulent gaze met hers, each time her heart cried out for him, she sent a prayer for help heavenward.

That evening, after work, she treated Gracie to a meal out before they went to the church for the choir's Christmas cantata. In the darkened sanctuary, while her daughter announced the good news to shepherds in the fields, Ellie saw Wyatt with Cade and Albert in the back pew. She silently wept but made no attempt to speak to him.

This time she would wait for God to work things out. At least she'd learned that much.

Chapter Fifteen

Christmas Eve.

"We need to go shopping, guys," Wyatt told Cade and Albert.

"Good, because thanks to the allowance you gave me I can buy a gift for Gracie." Albert grinned and wiped Cade's face. "And this guy."

Gifts? Wyatt almost groaned, realizing he had nothing to put under the tree for either Albert or Cade. And what in the world could he possibly give to Gracie and her mom?

"I was thinking of groceries," he said. "Can't have Christmas without groceries." *Or Ellie.* "But we can hit the mall, too. I was also wondering if you'd mind watching Cade later while I visit my mother?"

"Sure." Albert asked in a much quieter voice, "Can we stop by Ellie's, too?"

"Of course." So after some grocery shopping

and a mall stop, Wyatt pulled into the parking lot at Eventide. His mother seemed to recognize him, and after accepting a bouquet of flowers, she began a rambling series of memories revolving around his first Christmas. When she finished, Wyatt seized his opportunity.

"I brought you a Christmas gift, Mom," he said, using the word for the first time.

He pulled out the small tattered box that held a locket he'd purchased many years ago when he'd still believed his mom would someday come home. He handed it to her, feeling a bittersweet delight when she enthused over the gift. Inside he'd placed two pictures, one of him as a child and one of Cade.

After staring at those pictures for several moments, Ruth suddenly changed. She fidgeted and grew increasingly agitated as she muttered about having to leave. The attendant arrived, and Wyatt knew that was his cue to go. So he kissed her cheek, wished her a Merry Christmas, then collected Albert and Cade from the gathering room, realizing that he'd just spent the first Christmas he could remember with his mom.

Back in his truck, he closed his eyes while Albert buckled in Cade, praying for—what, he didn't know. Help, perhaps, to deal with his uncertain future.

"When will we go to Ellie's?" Albert asked after a long silence.

"I think she'll still be at work. Let's go home and give your bowl one last oiling before you give it to her." He couldn't see her yet, not like this, not while his emotions were so ragged.

But back at home, time didn't help, because everywhere Wyatt looked he saw Ellie's hand. The huge box of baking that now sat inside his porch could only be from her. The decorations that made his home look so festive. The tree she'd helped him decorate when he realized he was trying too hard to be his father's son. Even the bowl Albert carefully wrapped showed Ellie was tied into his life with bonds not easily broken.

Wyatt desperately wanted to run to her, to let her love him, to love her back. But one thing stopped him. Fear of the future. He could not, would not, saddle her with the responsibility of raising Cade, Gracie and maybe even Albert, alone. That was one promise he intended to keep, no matter how much it hurt.

"Wyatt?" Albert stood before him with two glasses of milk and a plate of Ellie's gingerbread cookies. "Cade's napping, so I thought—I wondered—did you always have happy Christmases like this?"

Happy?

"Not always." But Albert pressed, and finally Wyatt began recounting details. Somehow the pain from his past came pouring out.

When he eventually stopped, Albert remained silent for a long time, then said, "I think your father was hard on you because he was trying to protect you."

Taken aback, Wyatt frowned. "Why do you think that?"

"Isn't that what fathers do, what parents do, what everyone does? They protect the special people in their lives as best they can. Because they love them. That's what Gran did for me." Albert munched on another cookie before he continued. "That's what God as our Father does for us. That's what Ellie does. Even Gracie's trying to protect her mom by searching for a daddy who will love them."

Surprised by the depths of Albert's thinking, Wyatt could only listen.

"Learning about your mom made you realize how alone you are." Albert nodded sagely. "It was like that for me when Gran got sick. I knew she was going to die and that then I'd be all alone. I was so scared."

He marveled at Albert's wisdom, the poise he showed in his words, and was reminded of a verse he'd read. *A child shall lead them.*

"What did you do?"

Albert gulped his milk before he replied. "I remembered what she'd taught me, that God is always there, always protecting me, no matter what happens. When my uncle got mean I remembered a verse she'd taught me when I was little. I must have said 'I will not fear' a thousand times while I waited for God to protect me." Albert grinned, his milk mustache comical. "And here I am."

"It's not quite—"

"The same?" Albert finished. "Sure it is. Because that's what you're doing for Ellie and Gracie by pushing them away. You're trying to protect them. That's what love does. And you love them. Don't you?"

Those words gave Wyatt a glimpse of his future—sad and empty without Ellie and Gracie, brimming with joy with them in it.

Albert put down his milk. "I think you're protecting them the wrong way," he said.

"You do?" Intrigued, Wyatt looked up at the boy.

"Uh-huh." Albert studied him. "See, Christmas is all about love and giving. That's what God showed us when He gave the gift of His son at Christmas." He finished his cookie. "I think God was saying that with His love we can deal with anything."

Though Wyatt detested milk, he realized he'd

drunk the entire glass as he mulled over Albert's words.

With God's love we can deal with anything.

Even schizophrenia?

That meant he'd have to trust God with the unknown. Trust God to help him share whatever future he could forge with Ellie and Gracie. But what was the alternative? Go it alone and miss out on really living, really loving? Throw away everything he wanted in his world?

Become like his father?

No.

It took every ounce of faith Wyatt could dredge up to make the decision.

Okay, God. I'm trusting You.

Overwhelming relief told him he'd made the right choice.

"Albert, I need to go shopping," he said as he jumped to his feet.

"Again?" Albert groaned, then rose. "Okay. But after that, can we go to Ellie's?"

"Absolutely." Wyatt's heart thrummed with anticipation as he drove to the mall. He left Albert pushing Cade in his stroller while he went inside a store and found two gifts that exactly met his needs.

Then they drove to Ellie's. He'd been so stupid to push her away. Ellie had said she loved him. After his colossal mistake, would she still?

"We'll stay in the car so you can have some privacy." Albert grinned. "Not that you'll get much with Gracie there."

Wyatt thanked him and walked to the door. Pushing out a ragged breath, he knocked.

He was prepared to plead his case with Ellie. He was not prepared for a little girl clad in a pair of red jeans and a white T-shirt wearing a green felt elf's hat that flopped over one eye to open the door.

"Hi, Gracie. Is your mommy here?" Boy, had he missed this kid.

"She's in the shower. Why? Are you gonna make her cry again?" Gracie glared at him.

"No, I, uh—" Wyatt had to do something fast to change this situation, or nothing would go as he wanted. "Actually I was hoping I could talk to you first."

"Why?" she demanded.

He knelt on one knee, right there at the door, and looked straight at her. "Because I was wondering…if your mom agrees to marry me, could I be your daddy?"

Gracie shoved back the hat, her blue eyes wide. She gaped at him then breathed, "Really?"

"Absolutely. If your mom agrees. Because I love her, and I want to marry her. That means I'd be marrying you, too." He took a breath. "But I make an awful lot of mistakes, and sometimes I break my promises and—"

"That's okay." She grinned. "Me an' Cade an' Albert will help you get better 'cause we love you."

"I love you, too, Gracie. So will you marry me?" he asked formally.

"Sure." She nodded, her happy smile stretching across her face.

"Thank you. I'm going to make you one promise that I'll never break. I'll always love you, Gracie. As long as I live." Wyatt lifted her hand, pressed a kiss in her palm, then slid a tiny ring with a topaz stone on to her finger. "This is to remind us of my promise to love you always."

"Wow." Gracie lifted her hand to stare at her ring. "Are we 'gaged?" she whispered.

Wyatt nodded and kissed her forehead. "We certainly are."

"Gracie?" Ellie's voice echoed from inside the house.

Wyatt put his finger to his lips. "But you have to keep it a secret until I ask your mom. Okay? Can you do it?" he begged.

"Sure." Gracie turned and yelled, "Mommy, Da—somebody's here to see you." She winked at him. "'Cause I can't call you Daddy yet," she whispered.

"Gracie Grant, you know very well you are

not to open the door—Oh." Ellie appeared, her hair a mass of damp curls. She wore an outfit matching Gracie's, except her hat bore a white fur band. "Hello," she said in her coolest voice.

"Gracie, may I talk to your mom alone?" Wyatt thought he'd never seen anyone so lovely as his Ellie. *Don't let me botch this, God.*

"'Kay." Grace shot him an outrageous wink, then raced away.

"Ellie, I—"

"Merry Christmas, Wyatt. I hope you, Cade and Albert have a happy day." Her cool gray eyes gave away nothing.

Wyatt immediately revamped his approach.

"Thank you for the baking you left. I have your gift here," he said and held out the black velvet ring box. When she didn't take it, he flipped it open to show her the diamond solitaire sitting inside. "Ellie, will you marry me?"

Ellie's gaping stare swiveled from the ring to him, back and forth, confusion filling her face. "Why?"

"Because I love you. I need you in my life." Wyatt's heart welled with emotion. "I have no idea whether or not I will end up as my mother. I have no guarantees to offer you except that, for as long as I breathe, I will love you and do my utmost to cherish you."

"But you said—"

Wyatt touched her cheek, unable to keep his hands away from her. This beautiful woman was what he wanted in his life. Her love meant his world would be whole, complete.

"I forgot, Ellie," he whispered. "I forgot that God is in charge of my world, and He'll decide my future. I forgot that I need to trust that He will do His best for me." He took her hands in his and pressed the ring box into her palms. "What I finally realized today, thanks to Albert, is that any moment I have with you is more precious than years without you. Because I love you and that's a precious gift from God. So, will you marry me, Ellie Grant, and make Gracie's Christmas wish come true?"

"Yes," she said simply and with heartfelt emotion. She held out her hand for him to slide on her ring. "Because I love you, Wyatt. You are God's answer to me. I'll grab whatever time we have together to share with our kids and whomever else He brings into our paths. Because I love you."

His heart brimming with joy and thanksgiving, Wyatt embraced her. With slow deliberateness he kissed her, pledging his love to her for as long as he lived.

And Ellie kissed him back, at least until a voice came from behind Wyatt.

"Do you think Cade and I can come in now? He needs a diaper change."

Wyatt and Ellie glanced at Albert and burst out laughing.

"By rights, you should have to change him since you're going to be his brother," Wyatt teased.

"Hmm. Something to think about. Merry Christmas." Albert handed Ellie her bowl and Wyatt his son. "Where's Gracie?"

"In here," she called out. "Looking at the 'gagement ring my daddy gave me."

Ellie's eyebrows arched as she glanced at Wyatt.

"I hope you don't mind that I asked Gracie to marry me first," he said as he ushered her inside and closed the door. "And I should have mentioned something else."

"Oh?" In between sneaking glances at her ring, Ellie gave him a wary look.

"I don't know what will happen in the future, darling Ellie, but I intend to keep working at Wranglers Ranch as their staff veterinarian because that's where I belong."

"I know what will happen in the future," she said as she pressed a kiss against Cade's head and then Wyatt's cheek. "What will happen is that I will love you, and you will love me, and together we'll work at Wranglers, showing kids what God's love is all about. Right?"

"Lady, you are so right." Wyatt turned his head just the tiniest bit to kiss her again, thrilled by what his future held as long as she was by his side.

"Mommy, Albert wants me to open my gift. An' I want Cade to open his giant nutcracker cookie. 'Kay?"

"Wait till we're all there, sweetie. We'll open them together." Ellie nudged Wyatt toward the bathroom. "You can change Cade in there. After we open gifts, we're going to Wranglers. They're having a staff campfire, and I can't wait to share our news."

"Excellent idea. Christmas Eve together with friends. How can it get better?"

But as they sat around a campfire later, singing carols, Wyatt knew in the depths of his heart that it would get better. Because God so loved the world that He gave His only son.

That was the message he and Ellie and their family would help Wranglers Ranch spread.

He clung to his fiancée's hand, ready to face their future with God in charge.

* * * * *

If you enjoyed this story, pick up the first
WRANGLERS RANCH *book,*
THE RANCHER'S FAMILY WISH
and these other stories from Lois Richer:

A DAD FOR HER TWINS
RANCHER DADDY
GIFT-WRAPPED FAMILY
ACCIDENTAL DAD

Available now from Love Inspired!

Find more great reads at
www.LoveInspired.com

Dear Reader,

Welcome back to Wranglers Ranch where life's so busy an on-staff nurse and veterinarian are necessary. But these two single parents aren't interested in finding someone to love. It's going to take some strong-minded love to bring Ellie and Wyatt together. Fortunately there's a little girl determined to get a daddy for Christmas whether or not it's on her mom's list.

I hope you've enjoyed Wyatt and Ellie's struggle to understand God's love is always there, waiting for us to come home to it. Join me next time at Wranglers Ranch where you're always welcome.

I love to hear from you: write me via Facebook, www.loisricher.com, loisricher@gmail.com or snail mail at Box 639, Nipawin, SK S0E 1E0, Canada.

I wish you a Merry Christmas as together we celebrate the greatest gift ever given. May His love penetrate your heart and soul as you move toward a future He has prepared just for you.

Blessings,

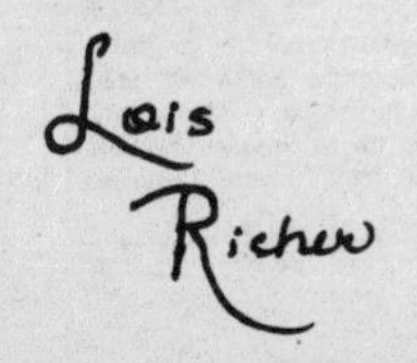